I0554450

Agent of Salt

Rachel Anne Jones

I dedicate this story to Douglas—always and to my friends and family.
Thank you for your continued support.

"You don't need a book to learn what to do with a man..."

— Big Stone Gap, Adriana Trigiani

one

"Gimme a Bud Light," Caden Brown says as he slaps down his credit card and prepares to belly up to the bar to watch the basketball game from his favorite bar stool, the one with the asymmetrically cracked seat cushion that gives in all the right places beneath his 187-pound, six-foot two-inch build. It's close enough to the corner TV he can hear the sportscaster in one ear and whomever he's talking to in the other. Having a cold beer on his favorite stool isn't everything, but it'll make up for the crap week he's just had despite being promoted to salt mine foreman twenty-two days ago, which had him shopping for Docker's and button-up shirts and tossing his bagged-up stained jeans and mining jacket to the back of his closet.

Caden was thrilled with the promotion that he never thought he'd get. He recalls the last day of riding the elevator up out of the mine. He was so happy he was doing a Travis Kelce dance-of-joy for all his haters that said he'd never make management inside his head. He can't believe he already has the urge some days to go back down below. Desk jobs can be a real headache, and today was no exception. He grabs his Bud and walks toward his seat, but someone slides in first.

Caden pauses and reminds himself he's a grown man and that he doesn't own a bar stool despite the fact he's been sitting on it for two years straight every Friday night between the hours of 7:30PM and 9:30 or 10:30 PM, depending on who's bartending, who walks in, and if there's good conversation. Caden searches for Owen, his favorite bartender because he's the friendliest and never short on interesting topics, but there's someone else, someone he doesn't know.

"Terrific. The hits just keep comin'," he mumbles while he plops down a bar stool two stools down from the one he wants, just in case the stool-stealer with his back turned to him moves. Caden takes a long draw from his beer, hoping it'll cool his irritation.

Jeri White leans on the corner of the bar, wishing she'd never let her co-worker Charmaine talk her into going out on a Friday night to some no-name smalltown bar in a mining town no less, chasing down some random TikTok hottie.

"You don't even know if he lives here anymore," Jeri whines in Charmaine's ear, which is hard to do through all the decoration. Charmaine's got so much metal in her ear Jeri's sure she'd set off the metal detector at an airport. "Who knows how old that TikTok is."

Charmaine turns on her. "Gir-l, quit your whinin'. It's Friday night. We ain't gotta work tomorrow."

Jeri supposes she's right, but she's annoyed. "I could be home right now watching Dateline," she grumbles.

Charmaine makes bug eyes at her friend. "DVR your stupid show. That TV can't compete with a memory. We might meet a famous TikTok'er tonight," she says with a voice full of hope.

Jeri feels bad for trying to pop her friend's happiness bubble, but sometimes Charmaine's misplaced enthusiasm is exhausting, especially because most of it is tied to the nightlife. Meeting guys under the influence of dim lights and alcohol has never seemed like the best idea to Jeri. Charmaine hikes up her already-short skirt before hauling her vertically challenged self onto the high barstool. She proceeds to rest her *girls* on the bar. Jeri's relieved to see colorful booty shorts underneath her friend's hiked-up skirt. Her eyes pop when she spies Charmaine's red satin bra peeking out of the single-buttoned cropped cardigan.

"Do your booty shorts match your bra?" Jeri asks a little too loud.

Caden chokes on his beer and looks in their direction. He gives the curvaceous sister a bold wink before checking out the awkward loudmouth hiding behind her. All he sees of the louder-than-necessary blonde is her plain-colored shirt and long dark sweater. He leans back just enough to see if he can see anything of her legs, but they're covered up by some formless skirt that almost hits the floor.

His eyes meet hers. She stares straight at him, but her look is not the usual look of appreciation he gets when a woman looks in his direction. Before he knows it, he's off his stool. He swaggers a little more than usual just to piss her off. From the growing scowl on her face, he'd say it's working.

He zeroes in on the barely-covered sister. She looks much friendlier. "You're new here. Can I buy you a drink?" he offers in a casual tone.

Before she can answer, the tiny nondescript blonde

beside her shakes her head. "No, we were just leaving," she says. Her voice is a little low for a woman, but at least it's not squeaky.

The vibrant sister beside him lays a hand on his arm. Her nails are long and jeweled. Caden doesn't care for high maintenance, but he's curious to see if he can make the blonde jealous. He stays where he is.

"I'm Charmaine. We can stay for a drink," the sister says as she bats her bright purple eyelashes at him. She gestures toward the scowling blonde. "This is Jeri."

Caden gives Jeri a flirty wink and a come-hither smile. She scowls even harder. He didn't think that was possible. He resists the urge to laugh. He turns back to Charmaine.

"What's the deal between you two? Is she like your parole officer?" he teases.

Charmaine laughs out loud. "I've been called a lot of things, but never a criminal," she says with an open smile. "That's pretty good."

Caden can't figure them out, but he likes Charmaine. She's funny. "I don't think your friend likes me very much," he teases.

Charmaine giggles. "She's all work and no play." She drags a nail down the inside of his forearm and leans forward. Caden didn't think her top could get any bigger. He resists the urge to scoot back. "I don't mind a little of both," she teases.

The blonde drops her phone face-up on the bar with a clatter. She taps her middle finger on the screen in a pointed manner. "Do you know this man?" she demands.

Caden gives her an exasperated look. He picks up the phone and squints at it, turning it this way and that. He knows exactly who it is. He's just enjoying seeing her get all sorts of worked up. He keeps her phone until she puts her palm out with a glare. Caden doesn't understand himself or the need to touch her, but he thinks it has something to do with wanting to rattle her cage. He sets his beer down and takes a hold of the underside of her hand before laying the phone down in her palm. He keeps his hold.

"What'll you give me if I do?" he asks in a suggestive tone. Her cheeks pinken. This makes him feel better than he'd like to admit. He can't believe he's attracted to a woman who dresses and acts like a grandma.

Jeri whips her business card out of her pocket and slaps it on the bar before jerking her hand and phone away from his hold that sends more shocks of heat through her than she'd like to admit. "There's my number. Give me a call day or night," she barks before spinning around so fast she bumps elbows with her friend who falls against Caden.

Caden keeps his eyes on the card while he waits for Charmaine to right herself. "She's a bail bondsman?" he says in a voice of disbelief. He would have pegged her for a schoolteacher or an accountant, what with all the stuffiness in her tone and the rest of her being as rigid as a 2x4.

Charmaine exhales slowly. Her warm manner cools. "She's got you, don't she," she teases in a light-hearted manner. She taps her jeweled nails on the bar. "So who's the TikTok guy? I'm the one who's lookin' for 'em."

Caden can't believe how relieved he is to hear the blonde isn't chasing after Tony, the TikTok'er who put their tiny town of Michigan on the map. "He's in L.A." he says. Charmaine's face falls. He feels kind of bad. "You still want that drink?" he offers.

She pats him on the arm. "Nah, but thanks anyways. If I don't follow her out, she's liable to leave me."

The tiny blonde bun pops back up beside Charmaine. She's so close she almost bumps into Caden. In this light, she looks much younger. Her fair skin is flawless. Her lips are just the right shade of pink. He wishes he could make her smile. "You came on awful strong with that line. It's kinda agro," he teases, trying to see if she has a sense of humor.

Her glare intensifies. "I wasn't hitting on you," she growls before poking him in the chest. "Trust me, before the end of the night, you'll be callin' me from behind bars. I can spot recklessness a mile away. You're not my type. You should have stuck with Charmaine."

His jaw drops. He can't believe how rude she's being. He glances at Charmaine. She shrugs her shoulders and gives him a saucy smile.

He takes a long swig of beer. He can't believe how judgmental Jeri is, or how much it turns him on. "Honey, I wouldn't call you if I was sittin' in a jail cell and you were the only bail bondsman in a two-hundred-mile radius," he growls right back.

Jeri gives him her cheesiest smile. "We'll see about that," she says before puckering up and blowing him a noisy kiss as she backs away. "I always get my man."

Caden knows she's being a smart ass, but her little act steals his breath. He watches her walk away, leaning into her friend. Her tight little bun doesn't move a hair as she tilts her head towards Charmaine's. They're probably laughing at him. Caden watches the sway of her skirt as it flirts with the floor. Charmaine's skirt barely covers her booty. Caden can hardly believe an insulting, uptight woman dressed like a church lady is the one who has him starin'.

He shakes his head to clear it and stomps back to the empty barstool that's not his. "She thinks she's so smart. She

6

doesn't know me. There's no way I'm spendin' the night in jail. I've never even broken the law," he grumps.

"Caden, Is that you? No way," a voice booms. Caden fights the urge to duck and cover as he turns slowly toward the right to affirm he should've left right after Jeri and all her sass made such a memorable exit. He pastes a surprised look on his face as he catches Bairn's eye.

"Hey, man. What's up?" Caden asks Bairn Barnes, an old junior college teammate, a guy he hasn't seen in two years. Caden tries to keep a straight face when it hits him the last time he saw Bairn was at another teammate's wedding dance. Bairn was so drunk he was incoherent. Caden was trying to figure out how to turn down an overly tipsy, newly-divorced Stephanie who was determined to walk him to his car when he accidentally stumbled upon Bairn lying face down drunk in the ditch on the way to the parking lot. Caden was never so relieved to toss Bairn in his car and drive off with him while pretending to not hear Stephanie yelling *call me* at him through his mostly rolled-up window.

"Not much, man," Bairn answers. "How have you been?"

"I've been alright. Just workin'," Caden answers in a bored tone he hopes implies he wants to be left alone so he can chill out, watch basketball, and forget all about the judgy little blonde woman who was as rigid and uptight as the neat little bun on the top of her head. He's never found gritchy women attractive, so what's so special about this one, he wonders.

"Hey. Remember when we played the game back in the day?" Bairn asks in a tone that tells Caden he's just getting started. Caden holds in a groan. Bairn never tires of reliving the glory days that never were, as far as Caden is concerned, and he's perfectly fine with it too. They went to a junior college. Ain't no shame in that, in Caden's opinion, but it also means there were never going to be any awe-filled moments that were going down in sports history or written on a plaque hung on a wall. Seven long minutes and fourteen points scored by the wrong team later on the corner TV that Bairn keeps blocking with his stupid baby face that's gone into full pout mode, and Caden has had enough.

"Dammit, Bairn, I'm tryin' to watch the game," Caden barks a little too loud about the time he sees Bairn's already red face grow even darker.

"I know, man. It was some game. We shoulda won it, and we would've, but someone paid the refs," he says as he slams his mostly empty beer on the bar. "It was so unfair. We got robbed."

Caden blinks. He's a little fuzzy from downing two more beers in the span of four minutes to try to block out Bairn's never-ending over-exaggerated recount of every game they ever played together, most likely, because that's how every conversation goes that comes out of his mouth. "Dude. I'm talkin' about the game on the TV," Caden grumps as he waves his arm past Bairn's left shoulder to point in the general direction.

Bairn's stares up at Caden through his beer haze. "Why do you care about that stupid game? It's not even the play-offs. I haven't seen you in forever. I thought we were catchin' up."

Caden knows it's foolish and a little cruel, but he's had enough. His favorite team just lost, and he missed the last five minutes because he had to listen to the same conversation he hears every time he and Bairn get together, which just became one time too many.

"We aren't catchin' up, Bairn. I'm sittin' here trying to

ignore you while you go on about your glory days that were never that glorious. I've worked a long week. I'm tired. I just want to sit here and enjoy my beer and the game before goin' home to a quiet apartment to chillax. I wasn't up for you sittin' on my stool, in my spot, blockin' my view with your stupid fat head." All the air goes out of Caden about the time Bairn sucks it up.

Bairn hops off the barstool. Caden feels bad because he thinks Bairn was probably taller when he was sitting on the stool. Bairn's chest puffs out. Caden's never figured out how Bairn can manage to look down on guys when he's shorter than most, a fact that wouldn't bother Caden a bit if Bairn weren't so obnoxious.

"You're lucky I know you're drunk, Caden, or I'd beat your ass right here, right now," Bairn threatens.

Caden knows he should either agree and walk out or let Bairn have his swagger just like every other time it's happened ever since they were little. Like when Bairn paid him twenty bucks to take the fall in a fake fight to impress a girl, because he thought that would cause brown-eyed art student Mia to fall fuschia-colored hair over her crazy patterned tights and mis-matched Converse for him.

Boy, was he wrong. Mia called Bairn a barbarian before giving Caden a shove on his way up out of the dirt at recess, muttering *idiots* under her breath at him, but she gave Caden a smile that told him she didn't believe for a minute Bairn could ever knock him on his butt. Her smile, although mostly fake, was more than Bairn got. Bairn's big mouth didn't do him any favors then, just like it isn't now, Caden thinks as he stands up to his full height of 6'2".

Caden stares down at Bairn, who had the unfortunate experience of having a mother who loved all things Scottish and didn't realize she was giving her only son a name that would stick with him all his life like a personality flaw. "I'm not drunk," Caden drawls in a tone as stiff and neat as the whiskey he's going to drink as soon as Bairn is out of his sight. "Not even close," he adds for good measure.

With all the experiences between them as teammates, Bairn ought to know Caden's patience is just about gone, because Caden's grammar improves the more irritated he gets. But anyone who knows Bairn knows he's as stubborn as an ass. He's got more pride than three men put together.

"What are you saying?" Bairn demands as his gray-blue eyes blink in rapid succession while he stares up at Caden, whose easy-going demeanor has all but disappeared, save for the tiny smirk that's impossible to miss.

"I know you heard what I said," Caden enunciates in a tone that is more of a reprimand, "and I'm not saying it again," he says as he starts to move past Bairn. "Now if you'll excuse me, I'm going to go to the *men's* room, a place you've yet to occupy," he taunts as he lays a light hand on Bairn's shoulder just as he passes by.

Bairn flings Caden's hand off his shoulder in a dramatic manner right before he punches Caden in his back left side. Caden doesn't think twice before reacting. He pivots on his foot and comes around with a right hook that slams into Bairn's dimpled chin. Down Bairn goes. Caden stands over an unmoving Bairn for too many seconds, but he's not worried. He knows Bairn all too well. He's perfected playing the victim. Besides, Bairn threw the first punch. Caden wants to leave, but he figures the least he can do is help Bairn up off the floor whenever he's ready to quit acting like a child.

Twenty seconds later, Bairn still hasn't moved. Caden leans over and nudges him in the side with the back of his hand. Bairn just lays there. Caden pokes him between the ribs. Bairn swats his hand away and groans. Caden throws his head back and laughs. He can't believe what a wimp Bairn is being. It was one thing for him to act like this in junior college on the basketball court when he was trying to get a technical called on the other team, but they're men now. Their seven-year high-school reunion is coming up as a reminder of that fact. Bairn's way too old to be playing opossum over a fight he himself started.

Caden still hasn't decided if he's going to the reunion. Over half of them are married and have started their families. Caden hasn't done either. He doesn't even have a girlfriend. He supposes he's always been a bit particular, but he's never been one to treat dating like a sport. He'd rather be alone than be with somebody just so he won't be alone. He feels slightly ridiculous that he's not embarrassed about being single, but he knows one thing—he's not spending the whole night of the reunion sitting around with Bairn, listening to him blather about the good old days.

Caden grabs a hold of Bairn by the upper arm. "C'mon man. Get up. You're makin' a fool of yourself."

Bairn shoves his hand away and makes a show of pushing himself up off the floor. "Why'd you do that? I thought we were friends," he whines.

Caden feels a little bad when he sees Bairn's split bottom lip and swelling chin, but not bad enough. It's not his fault Bairn has such a small face and Caden's hands are a bit big. "What are you talking about?" Caden demands. "You hit me first. I just reacted," he argues.

Bairn dabs at his lip with the bar napkin. "I tripped and fell into the back of you. It was an accident."

Caden rolls his eyes. "Whatever, man. You're still singin'

11

the same song, always blamin' someone else. Nothing is ever your fault."

Bairn's eyes water. Caden can't believe he's about to cry. "You're just jealous of me. You always have been. That's why you punched me," he accuses.

Caden shakes his head and taps his closed fist on the bar. "Whatever, man. Just keep tellin' yourself that if it helps. You're delusional."

Bairn's swollen lip pops out even more as he stares Caden down. "You'll be sorry you did this to me. Just you wait and see."

Caden takes another drink of his Bud Light as Bairn heads for the front door of the bar. "Yeah, okay. I've heard that one before," he yells at Bairn's retrieving back before turning around to the bartender. "Give me a whiskey, neat," he says.

The bartender raises a questioning eyebrow. "Are you sure?"

Caden nods. "Yeah, I'm sure. I haven't seen that guy in two years, and as soon as I do, I wish I hadn't. What a chump."

The bartender's only answer is to slide the whiskey across the bar in front of Caden who takes a sip before carrying it over to sit on the seat Bairn was just on. He shifts around until he hears the tiny crinkle beneath his right thigh. "That's more like it," he says with a smile before turning to read the bartender's nametag. "Hey, Jeff. Turn that game up, would ya?"

two

Jeri White slams down her desk phone on Monday morning. "If I hear one more fake medical excuse about another degenerate missing their court date after I bonded them out, I'm going to shut my *own* hand in the office door and miss work for a *real* accident," she declares as she eyeballs her desk mate. Charmaine delivers her famous signature eyeroll like only she can do. Charmaine's got the biggest brown eyes Jeri's ever seen.

"Girl, I know you playin'," Charmaine teases. "You're just feelin' salty about your bad date night last night." Jeri winces at her best friend's words. She doesn't mind the play-by-play of her non-existent love life, but Charmaine is hell on cross-examination. "What'd you do to him this time?" she demands.

Jeri shrugs her shoulders. "I don't know what you're talking about," she says, but she's not fully committed to her defense. Charmaine leans in on her elbows. Her sweater dips of its own volition. "Tuck those things back in before they fall out on my desk," Jeri warns.

13

Charmaine giggles as she tugs at her top. "Girl, that ain't me. That's the laws of gravity."

Jeri raises an eyebrow. "You sure you got the right bra size?"

Charmaine raises a coffin nail to her chin and taps. "Let me think...um, yeah, they gave me the largest bra there is. Some things just can't be contained," she teases as she jiggles her front about the time the new mail boy walks by. He trips over his feet and manages to catch himself before going to the floor, but he's not quick enough to stop the mail from flying everywhere. Jeri shoots Charmaine a look of warning. She's too busy making her *it's not my fault* face to notice as she turns back to bargain shopping on Amazon for another sweater for her pet Yorkie, Boo. She catches Jeri's look of disgust in her reflection in the computer monitor.

"That dog of yours has more sweaters than me," Jeri scolds.

"We live in northern Michigan. We have long winters. My Boo gets cold," Charmaine argues. "Besides, you're one to talk, cardigan lady. You've got more sweaters than my gramma."

Jeri sniffs. "Whatever. At least I don't wear sweaters that look like someone forgot to knit the rest of them. You do realize you didn't walk off the set of *Outer Banks*, right?" Jeri says before giving Charmaine a withering look.

"You been watchin' Netflix with your niece again, haven't you," Charmaine teases. "And now you think you all cool with the little homies."

Jeri raises her finger. "All I'm saying is, I would hope any kid who watches that show knows it's nothing like real life. There's no hidden treasure waiting to be discovered. And there's no guys..." she stops, feeling embarrassed.

Charmaine giggles. "No guys what? No guys you know who look like those little pogue hotties?"

Jeri exhales slowly. "You know what? This is a stupid conversation, and it's officially over."

Charmaine giggles some more. "Ooh, girl. Which one you like? Blonde-haired JJ or hazel-eyed John B who runs like a girl? The boy is a little too graceful to be hot."

Jeri pffts. "And I suppose you think Pope is hot."

Charmaine snaps her fingers and bobs her head just a little. "Girl, you know it. That brotha's hair is as thick as those beautiful lips of his. And he's sweet to his mama. They ain't get no better than that."

Jeri rolls her eyes. "Now who's getting all over the moon for a TV character?" She stares at her pile of future court dates, trying to get psyched up to start making phone calls. She feels Charmaine's eyes on her. "What?" she asks as she looks her friend in the eye.

"What was wrong with your date last night?" Charmaine demands.

Nothing, Jeri thinks to herself. Nothing except there was no spark. Nothing besides the fact she caught him checking out other women at least three times. He didn't even try to hide it. "He definitely wasn't a John B," she says with a small smile on her face.

Charmaine laughs out loud. "Oh, girl. I knew it. You like the strong, silent type. Ones that don't have time for small talk because they so focused." She eyes her friend. "Kinda like that guy we met at the bar the other night. He was hoot."

Jeri frowns. "Focused is just another word for boring," she grumps. She blushes when she remembers how much his touch on the back of her hand affected her. Or was it the way his eyes twinkled when he looked at her? "He wasn't that hot," she argues.

Charmaine's eyes bug. "Um, yes, he was. I'd wrap that boy up like a burrito just to take a bite."

Jeri can't help but giggle. "You know you sound crazy."

Charmaine gives her an ornery grin. "I'm just sayin'. The boy had it goin' on. I know you saw it." She points a ring-covered index finger at Jeri. "And focused ain't boring. It sounds like you," she teases. "You sayin' you're boring?"

Jeri leans back in her seat before alphabetizing her stack of criminals. "So what if I am?" Jeri defends herself. "There's nothing wrong with that," she continues. "I prefer to talk turkey. So what?"

Charmaine sticks her tongue out. "And how many gobblers have you met so far?"

Jeri wiggles a finger beneath her chin. "This is a decent-sized city. I'm sure there are more than a few available turkeys. I just have to find them." She smirks at Charmaine. "They're not exactly parading around, fanning their feathers."

Charmaine wrinkles her nose at her friend. "Just when I think you might have a chance at gettin' a guy, you go and say something like that. You gotta check that country girl upbringin' at the door if you ever want to meet someone." She visibly shivers. "It's creepy."

Jeri picks up a piece of paper and waves it around. "So I should trade in my turkey callers for a coupla spray cans and start graffitiing my number on walls as a way to advertise I'm twenty-six and still single. I'll just tag it *desperate white girl needs a date. Call me*," she says in a dry tone.

Charmaine gets the giggles all over again. "We do live in

Michigan. The odds of you meeting a white boy are definitely in your favor."

Jeri stares down at the latest case to fall on her desk. "Yeah, like I'd ever meet a decent guy at work. I'm a bail bondsman."

Charmaine claps her hands. "Ooh, girl. You gone and done it now. Never say *ever* or *never*. That's when things start to happen." She purses her lips and widens her eyes. "And we ain't no bail bondsman. We are agents of Quan."

Jeri shakes her head and laughs. "Show me the money," she says while waving her hands around all dramatically. "Speaking of which, the guy last night sure didn't."

Charmaine raises her eyebrows. "Say what? Your problem was he didn't spend enough money?" She looks her friend up and down. "Girl, if you're turnin' gold digger on me, at least spice it up. You're gonna have to glam *way up* if you expect a man to break out his Gold card."

Jeri wrinkles her nose at her friend's suggestion. "Um, gross?" She exhales slowly. "I don't think it's asking too much to expect more than a single appetizer and two glasses of water. That hardly constitutes supper."

Charmaine pffts. "Maybe he was on his way to the gym or somethin'," her voice drops off.

Jeri groans. "Trust me, he wasn't. He's just cheap. He told me to meet him there. He showed up in an Uber and when he realized it wasn't going anywhere between us, he asked me to pay for half of our appetizers."

Charmaine gives her a small nod. "Okay, girl. I agree. That's pretty sad. What a tool." She cocks her head to the side. "What was his name?"

"Brian King," Jeri answers even as knows she'll probably regret telling Charmaine his name. She's a social media queen. Charmaine's innate ability to smoke out the sneakiest of criminals and cheapskates over the Internet never ceases to amaze Jeri, who still prefers to get her man the old-fashioned way, by telephone or in person. There's just something more personal about hearing a man's voice.

"Bri-an? His name is Bri-an?" Charmaine declares while pronouncing it like A-a-ron. "That's half the problem right there. I bet he spells it with the letter I."

Jeri chokes down her laughter. "What difference does it make how he spells his name?"

Charmaine shakes her head back and forth. "Girl, I don't know, but trust me, it do. There's just something about them names spelled with an *I*. They do somethin' to a guy's character." She peeks around her monitor to stare Jeri down. "He ain't no King neither. A name don't make you who you are, Jeri, and a man don't neither."

Jeri holds up a piece of white paper. "Okay, okay. Chill out. I surrender. I will not date any more Bri-ans."

Charmaine snaps her fingers once and does her little head bob. "Dang right you won't."

Jeri digs through her stack of papers, grumbling as she goes. "Maybe Mom's right. Maybe it's time for me to find a different line of work."

Charmaine raises a perfectly shaped eyebrow in question while staring Jeri down. "And leave me hangin'? You can't do that. We're a team. We're like Cagney and Lacey minus the bad eighties' hair."

Jeri laughs. "We're bail bond agents. We are not cops. I'm not about to slap cuffs on a guy" she quips.

"Speak for yo'self. I ain't gonna say I got no cuffs," her co-worker says with a saucy look on her face.

Jeri wrinkles her nose. "Um, please stop. I need a second cup of coffee if you're going there."

"They fuzzy and pink," Charmaine says with a wink. "Playful," she teases.

Jeri makes a barfing sound.

Girls Like You by Maroon 5 goes off. Charmaine gives Jeri a look. "Ooh, I've gotta call." Seconds later, she's up out of her seat and across the room with her phone to her ear "No, I will not take anything less than ten percent. The Judge said what? Well, that's not my problem. Don't whine at me 'bout that. The jail cell is yo' problem. Rodriguez, don't *act* like you don't know the drill. We done been down this road a few times already." There's a pause and silence. "Well, then hit up another uncle. You've got 'bout a dozen of 'em." She turns back to roll her eyes in an exaggeration at Jeri before stomping her foot. "Yo. Holla at me, boy, when you got the money," she says before she hangs up. Charmaine lingers in the doorway she's been standing in for the past three minutes. "I'm a go for a coffee. You want some?"

"No thanks. Your phone call got me all wound up," Jeri teases. "You sure are hard on Rodriguez."

Charmaine makes a clicking sound with her tongue. "Girl, you just said you wanted a second cup of coffee."

"No. I said if you're gonna talk about cuffs I need a second cup. We changed the subject. We're talking about repeat-offender Rodriguez. Keep up," she says as she makes bug eyes.

"Shoot, that boy done been to prison 'bout three times now in four years. And every time he act like he don't know what to do to get out." Charmaine shakes her head. "Aw-ight, I'll be back in a lil' bit."

"Your leather's squeaking," Jeri yells at Charmaine right

before the door shuts. Jeri rolls her eyes and leans back in her chair. "Leather skirts and half sweaters. It looks cute on her, but it's not for me. If that's what I gotta wear to get a man, I think I'll stay single," she mutters to her computer.

Jeri stares at her computer screen, trying to get motivated for the day. She pulls up her last pay stub, noting the sixty-two unused days of vacation. "Mom always said to save for a rainy day, so that's what I'm doing. There's nothing wrong with being a good worker," she says to herself. She stares at the picture on the wall, the one of a sandy beach beside miles and miles of blue ocean. A tiny red crab has one clawed foot in the air as if to say *come join me.* Jeri stares at his beady little eyes. "I wish I could, Mr. Crab. I wish I could."

"You talking to creatures on the wall now, Jeri?" he says from somewhere behind her. Jeri refuses to be embarrassed when she's caught talking to herself by her cheating ex, Miles. Well, almost.

"What're you doing here?" she asks as she does a half spin.

He slaps a check in the middle of her desk amidst her piles of paperwork. "I need a favor."

She gives him the stink eye. "What makes you think I'd do you any favors?"

He perches on the corner of a desk, looking like Mr. Cool in his three-piece suit and hundred-dollar haircut, a confident move that used to drive her crazy in a good way before he went and ruined the most perfect relationship she'd ever been in. They had nine months of bliss before she caught him in the mail room with Symphony, the temp, who probably didn't know her own zip code, let alone how to sort them.

"It involves money," he teases.

20

She eyes the check, counting three zeroes as she leans a little closer before she does the same to him. "Is it going to bounce?"

He does his best to look offended, but she doesn't break her searching gaze. "No, Jeri. It will clear. Geez. What do you take me for?"

She picks it up and gives it a thorough looking over. "What do you take me for is the fairer question," she muses.

He stares at her. She stares right back. He sighs louder than necessary. "Fine. Since you're not going to ask, I'll just tell you."

She snorts. "Honesty? Really? There's a first."

He ducks his head. "It's for a friend."

"Mmm, o-kay. I've heard that before too."

His head pops up. "This is different."

She crosses her arm on her chest. "That sounds familiar."

He stomps his foot. "Are you going to let me talk?"

She leans back and bites her lip. "If you think you can stop sounding like my last boyfriend who was a total tool then yes. Please continue," she orders.

Miles blinks a few times and then opens his mouth. "Thank you," he says in a polite tone that insinuates he wasn't just insulted for being the jerk-faced liar that he is. "As I was saying, it's for a friend. He works in the salt mines. He got into a fight downtown at the bar, and they threw him in jail. It happened last Friday night. He's gotta be out by tomorrow, or he's going to lose his job."

She studies him. "If he's employed and so desperate, why didn't he call me himself?"

He laughs out loud. "Caden's as stubborn as they come. He'd sit in that cell for six months before he'd call for help."

She taps on the thousand-dollar check. "Why are you so eager to help him?"

Miles looks all sheepish. "I, um. I owe him a favor. If I get him out of jail, he can't hold it over my head."

She narrows her hazel eyes from behind her glasses. "So this is about you," she accuses.

He throws his hands in the air. "I'm bailing a guy out of jail, but sure, it's about me."

She smirks at him. "Fine. But you realize if he doesn't show up for court or whatever, it's on you to pay me the other nine thousand dollars."

He shrugs his shoulders and looks all chill. "Caden's reliable. He won't stand you up," he assures her, and she has to wonder how he can have so much confidence in a guy who got himself thrown in jail. She remembers the thousand dollars and gives him another dirty look. Miles pulls a look of innocence. "What? What'd I say now?"

Jeri stares him down. "I just *love* how you conveniently forget that we were sharing the rent for six months before you left and then I had to figure out how to pay the full amount by myself. You knew that I could barely afford it because of the budget we worked out to be able to live there. That was before I figured out you were a liar."

Miles shrugs. "You kicked me out, Jeri. Why would I pay for a place I'm not living in?" He studies his fingernails. "That's on you."

Jeri tries to count to ten in her head, but Miles and his stupid smirk get in the way. "I kicked you out because you cheated on me," she reminds him.

He stares at the floor. "Maybe next time don't put the lease in your name. You're just asking to be dumped on."

Jeri stomps her foot. "You are *unbelievable*. You're seri-

22

ously going to act like you don't remember crying on my shoulder about your bad credit and begging me to put the lease in my name?" She shakes her head. "That sad sob story of yours probably wasn't even true."

He gives her a grin. "You should be thanking me. I taught you a lesson."

She rolls her eyes and snatches up the check. "And what lesson would that be, Miles? That you're a lying jerk who justifies bad behavior by calling it something other than what it is?"

He winks at her before turning away to walk out the door. "Don't say I never gave you anything." He's almost to her office door when he hesitates. "Oh, he's over in the next town."

She stops in her steps. "That's like forty-five minutes away."

"I told you he was a miner," he says, as if that's a proper explanation for asking her to drive an hour to go pick up a guy in a small-town jail, something she detests. Small town cops are three times as chaotic as the cities and even more reluctant to release an inmate.

three

Caden sits in his cell, fuming. He can't believe he wasted his one phone call on Bairn, the guy who put him in here, but he honestly thought if he gave him a chance at redemption Bairn would take it. It probably didn't help that a minute into the conversation Caden threatened to put him in the hospital or worse if he didn't come down there and get his ass out of jail in the next twenty-four hours, at which point Bairn hung up the phone.

What's even more irritating is he can't believe little Miss Doom-and-Gloom, Prim-and-Proper from the bar predicted he'd be right where he is. That ticks him off worse than anything else.

Caden is still in shock over being taken downtown in the first place. He stumbled home from the bar Friday night, barely made it up his apartment stairs and into his place before falling face first into his couch until the next morning. He was woke up by someone banging on his door. Caden stood there in his holey tee shirt and flannel pants with one sock on and one sock off when the cops started reading him

24

his rights. Nausea hit him halfway through and he ran for the sink, dragging Jeremy behind him with a handcuff between them. He was one step away when he lunged for the silver basin, not seeing the knife Jeremy had his eye on.

Caden puked his guts up while being pinned sideways on the edge of the sink. He still managed to get most of it in the sink, which was not an easy feat. After his hurling spell ended, the Burdiek brothers led him down the hallway and out the front door of the apartment to the waiting cop car. Caden was confused as he sat in the back of their car with his hands cuffed behind his back. "What is going on?"

"You're under arrest for assault and battery," Jeremiah said as their eyes met in the rearview mirror.

Caden could hardly believe it. "Are you for real right now?" he asked before looking around the cop car for a hidden camera somewhere. He scooted over until he was right in the middle and could stare at them in the mirror. "This has to be a joke. Am I'm being punked?"

Jeremy turned to look at him from the passenger seat. "I assure you it is not."

Caden laughed again and leaned back in his seat. "I assure you it is not," he repeated in the same tone of voice as the cop.

Jeremy got mad at his parroting and shook his finger at Caden. "That's not funny."

Caden shifted around in his seat. "Did Bairn put you two up to this? I gotta say it's over the top. Even for him."

Jeremiah met his eyes in the mirror, and that's when Caden knew it wasn't a joke. "This is no joke. We are taking you to the police station. You're going to spend the night in jail. This is a very serious charge. It's a felony."

Jeremy pointed at his brother and partner in the driver's

seat. "Hey. That's enough yakking. You're not supposed to tell him all of that."

Jeremiah shrugged his shoulders. "Why? He's going to find out soon enough, and he already knows who filed the complaint against him."

Jeremy shoved his brother. "You don't know that. Who's to say he didn't beat up more than one person?"

Caden cleared his throat. "I didn't, okay. I didn't even want to punch Bairn in his stupid baby face. We were sittin' at the bar watchin' a basketball game. Well, I was watchin' the game. He was yakkin' in my ear. He wouldn't shut up about our junior college days and sports. I got tired of hearin' him so I told him to stop talkin'. Then I went to go to the bathroom because I drank three beers while tryin' to shut him out. He punched me in the back as I walked by. I didn't think. I reacted. I turned around and clocked him. It was stupid. I shouldn't have let him get to me. But that's all that happened. It shouldn't be a felony. The only thing I did wrong was think Bairn could take a punch like a real man instead of cryin' to the cops like a little baby."

Jeremiah met his gaze again in the mirror. "If that's what happened, dude, I'm sorry. Sounds like you didn't do much wrong, but he filed charges, and he's wearing a C-collar to protect and stabilize his neck. We gotta take you in."

Fear struck Caden right in the chest. All he could see was medical bills piling up that Bairn will try to get him to pay. "A C-collar? Really?"

Jeremiah nodded. "Yeah. He was having trouble getting words out. He said his tonsils hurt from being punched so hard."

Caden managed to have some coherent thoughts despite his terrific hangover. "That's the dumbest thing I've ever heard. You can't have damage to your tonsils from bein' knocked out. That's just stupid." The cop's eyes widened. "And I didn't knock him out. He was totally fakin'. He's always been a whiner. He over-exaggerates." He stomped his foot in the car. "All they have to do is a CT of his head to prove nothin' was hurt."

"Regardless, we have to take you in. It's a serious charge," Jeremy argued.

Caden leaned back in the seat and closed his eyes. "How long 'til I'm out? I have work on Monday."

Jeremy laughed at him, which only infuriated him further. "You have to bond out."

Caden turned and stared out the window. "I can get a grand easy. That's not the problem."

Jeremiah eyed him in the mirror. "Then what is the problem?"

Caden stared him down. "I didn't start the fight. He did. I'm not the guilty one. He is."

Jeremiah slowed down and turned into the parking space. "Hate to tell you, man, but he's the one wearing the C-collar and he's the one saying you knocked him out cold."

"Like I said, it's not my fault he can't take a punch," Caden grumbled.

"That may be true, but that's not a good defense," Jeremiah answered.

"Why do I need a defense?" Caden asked.

"Because you're going to talk to a judge before this is over. My suggestion is that you plead guilty. It'll give you the least amount of time. It might even get you probation," Jeremiah suggested.

Caden's brown eyes flew open. A few dark brown curls flirted with his right eyebrow. He blew a little air upwards to get them out of his face. They fell back down. "I have to see the judge," he reiterated.

The brothers nodded their heads. "Yeah," Jeremy said. "It's standard procedure for this type of charge."

"Do I get to plead my case?" Caden asked.

'I wouldn't suggest that. We've got a hanging judge. You'd be better off entering a guilty plea and living like a hermit for the next six months to a year. It'll suck, but at least you'll be out on bail, and you'll be employed," Jeremiah answered. Caden wasn't too worried. His dad's been friends with the judge for years, but he wasn't about to tell them that.

Saturday's conversation with the Burdiek brothers runs through Caden's memory to the best of his recollection. He knows he should call his father to bail him out, but he doesn't want to. He's too angry. He thought sitting in a cell for a few days would help him cool off, but it seems to have had the opposite effect.

The door swings open. "Caden, come on out," Rick, the prison guard, who was known as the over-sized town bully and hasn't changed much, orders.

Caden stands up from his bed. "I knew if I waited long enough someone would come to their senses," he muses as he strolls past the guard.

"Ha, that's real funny," Rick taunts. "Someone posted your bail."

Caden stops in his tracks. "Who?"

"Jeri White," Rick says.

Visions of the card pop up. "You gotta be kiddin' me," Caden replies.

Rick chuckles. "He is a she. She's a bail bondsman, and she's waiting on you, so get a move on."

Caden stops himself from punching the wall. "I know who she is. I didn't call her," he says as he turns back around.

Thick Rick grabs him by the upper arm. "Where are you going?"

Caden stays in one place. "I'm goin' back to my cell. I want someone else."

Rick jerks him forward. "She's here, and she's waiting on you," he repeats, "so let's get moving. I ain't got all day."

Rick opens a few more doors before they end up in the lobby. She stands off to the side, staring at the floor. She's wearing another long sweater. It covers the half of her that doesn't hide beneath her long skirt. Her hair is tied up in a neat bun, just like the other night. The only thing halfway interesting are her stylish boots that suggest a little rebel. Caden stares at her, willing her to look in his general direction.

"Jeri," Rick barks.

She lifts her head and faces the two of them before approaching. If there's any recognition from the other night at the bar, she hides it well. "Rick. How's it going?"

Rick squeezes Caden's arm. "Jeri, this is Caden. Caden, this is Jeri." He releases his grip and drops his hand. "There. I did my part."

Jeri tosses a hand on her hip. "Man of few words, I like it," she says in the same no-nonsense voice as the other night. She gives Rick a small smile. Caden wants to punch Rick in the face.

What is going on? She's not exactly feminine. Her matter-of-fact voice doesn't match her wide-eyed stare that hints of a teenage girl. Despite her youthful look, her demeanor is as serious as a nun in a habit. She hasn't changed a bit since the last time they met. No matter how much he tries, Caden can't ignore her. He knows he's staring, but he can't help it. Her hazel eyes are the perfect almond shape. Her turned-up nose with the lightest of freckles makes him want to tap the end with his finger, but the scowl on those perfect pink lips of her is what draws him in the most.

"I'll take you home and run over the rules with you. As soon as I hear from the judge, I'll let you know your court date and all of that." She rattles off everything so quick he can tell she's said it more than a few times. "Do you have a lawyer?" she adds.

He's still processing the first half of their conversation and the fact that she acts as if he's a perfect stranger and not someone she chewed out at the bar that she herself stood in. The more he thinks about the whole thing, the angrier he gets. Her words are all jumbled in his head.

"Why would I need a lawyer?" he asks as he follows her. She's already halfway across the room.

"Because of the charges," she says. "I wouldn't advise standing in front of the judge alone." He can't help but notice that's the second time he's heard those words, and they still rub him the wrong way.

"I didn't do anythin' wrong," he tells her as they stand outside.

She snorts as she crawls into a tin can of a car. He stands on the sidewalk, staring at her through the windshield. She leans out her window. "Do you need a ride or don't you? Sparky won't bite."

He steps off the sidewalk and opens the door of the pale, yellow car. He ducks down to look her in the eye. "I don't think I'll fit in here."

She rolls her eyes. "Only one way to find out. Now get in

before I change my mind and make you walk home. You live at least a couple miles from here."

Caden makes a show of sitting down in the seat and pulling his long legs in one at a time. "Good grief. I'm crunched up like a jack-in-the-box. You call this thing a car?"

She throws an arm around his seat and looks backwards. "Make all the fun you want. It gets forty miles to the gallon in the city and fifty on the highway if I don't drive over sixty." She pulls out onto the road before looking over at him. "So are you going to plead guilty or what?"

He sighs. "I'm so tired of hearing that. Why should I plead guilty when I didn't do anythin' wrong?"

She wrinkles her nose. "It makes no difference to me, but it's been my experience most men don't get an assault and battery charge unless they've done something." She eyes him. "You don't look like a man who beats on a woman, so..."

He sits up straighter in his seat. "You are *unbelievable*. The first time we met, you told me I'd end up in a jail cell. The second time—" He stops talking when he catches her look of triumph. "What?"

She glances over at him. "Were you or were you not just walking out of the local jail?"

He turns away from her and stares out the window. "That was just dumb luck on your part and extremely bad timin' on mine," he mumbles the last few words before turning back to stare her down. "Why would you accuse me of bein' a man who hits women?" he demands, but before she can answer, he continues with his tirade. "And are you tellin' me you would let a wife beater in your car? That's not exactly safe," he accuses, feelin' slightly judgy, but after what she's said to him up until this point, he's way past caring.

31

She wiggles in her seat. "To tell you the truth I don't normally give people rides home."

His chest tightens a little at her admission. He can't believe he's nervous, but it's in a good way. "Oh? Then why are you takin' me home?"

Her cheeks turn a little pink. "Well, it has something to do with the guy who paid your bail."

Caden can't believe he hasn't asked about that yet. "Who was it?"

It's not his imagination that she takes a deep breath. "Miles Smith."

Caden closes his eyes and groans. "*Miles,*" he says as if it's a curse word. He turns to look at her. "Last I heard the dude moved to the city. How the heck did he know I was in jail?"

She taps her fingers on the steering wheel. "Guess he was keeping tabs on you. All I know is he gave me a thousand-dollar check, so here I am."

"Is it too late to go back to jail?" he asks in earnest.

Her eyes widen at his statement. "Are you serious?"

He pounds a heavy fist on his thigh. "I really, really, don't want to owe him one is all."

She grips the steering wheel. "That's funny. He said he owed you a favor, and now you're even." She signals and starts to get over in the next lane. Caden doesn't think as he reaches over and jerks on her steering wheel just as a sports car flies by, honking his horn. She swallows hard. Her already pale face looks white as a sheet. "That guy must have floored it. I didn't see him, and I just checked my mirrors."

"He was in your blind spot. I'm just glad he didn't hit you," Caden says before putting his hands in his lap. "Sorry I grabbed your wheel."

Jeri can't believe how shook she is. "That's okay. I'm sorry I didn't see him coming."

Caden notices the trembling in her fingers. He clears his throat. "It's alright. No harm, no foul."

She nods and swallows hard again. "I'll just double back then, to get to your place."

His hand shoots out in front of her. "You could turn left up past the next light if you can get over. There's an alley way that'll get you going the right way on the one-way street." He thinks about what she said. "So do you know Miles?"

She's all too happy to keep her eyes on the road as she turns the corner, avoiding eye contact with him. "Um, yeah. He's my ex."

Caden's head jerks sideways. "No way."

Jeri tosses a hand in the air. "Yep, that's me. I'm the fool who fell for a cheater."

"He said *you* cheated," Caden argues.

Jeri turns to stare him down. "I didn't. I'm not a cheater."

Caden chuckles. "I should've known he was lyin'. He was so insistent about it, and I didn't even ask." Her jaw tightens. "I'm just sayin' that we're not that good of friends, you know? I don't share my relationship business with him. I can tell you that much," he adds.

She pulls into his back lot. "I can see that. You don't seem the type to share more than necessary with anyone," she says as she opens her door and hops out.

"What're you doin'?" he asks.

She points at the building. "I'm coming up to see your place," she responds as she wonders the same thing. It's not protocol for her to give him a ride home or follow him inside, especially uninvited, but all Jeri knows is she's not ready to walk away from him.

Caden feels strange as he walks down the sidewalk just a few steps ahead of Jeri, who follows along behind him. He likes her shoes and the way her eyes study him so thoroughly. Her clothes are a bit much. She dresses like a grandma, and he's not sure what that's about other than it makes it twice as hard to know what her age is. He can't believe she dated Miles, whom he dragged out of the mine at least a year ago, before the shaft they'd been working in collapsed. Miles was legitimately scared clean down to his toes, but he had every right to be. If Caden hadn't drug him away from where he fell, Miles would be like non-existent.

Caden feels bad that he almost regrets rescuing Miles from certain death. It's just ever since that day, Miles watched for an opportunity to pay Caden back so he doesn't owe him one. Caden told him from the first day it all happened that Miles didn't owe him anything, that it wasn't any big deal, that he knew if their roles were reversed, Miles would have rescued him. But Miles couldn't let it go. When Miles left the mines and moved to the city, Caden was never so relieved.

They walk up the front sidewalk in silence. Caden feels like he should apologize for his home not being as neat as it would be if he were expecting company but decides against it. He didn't exactly invite her over or inside for that matter, and it's not like it's anywhere near being a date. She's his bail bondsman, and he didn't even hire her.

Jeri takes in the blue and yellow Welcome mat with a big M on it in front of his door. She wipes her boots before stepping inside. There's no missing the blue and yellow couch cushions with big M's on them, or the strange-looking creature in the frame on the wall. "What's with all the M's?" she asks.

Caden stares at her as if she's lost her mind. "University of Michigan," he offers in explanation.

"You're talking about the college," she muses.

He tosses a hand on his hip. "Are you seriously telling me you don't know a Wolverine when you see one?"

She claps her hands. "Hugh Jackman?"

He ducks his head in a dramatic fashion. "Excuse me?" he questions before flopping down in the middle of his couch.

She tilts her head to one side. "Wolverine. From the X-Men," she says as she taps her toe.

He crosses his arms on his chest. "How can you live in the great state of Michigan and not know their college's mascots?" he teases.

She shrugs her shoulders. "I'm an import, and I've never been much of a sports girl," she states in an unapologetic tone as if she's bored.

He looks her up and down one more time. "So, where'd you come from? Kansas?"

She sways just enough that her long skirt moves with her like a bell. It reminds Caden of a quiet country church on a Sunday morning. He feels itchy. She fiddles with her earring and smiles a little smile that washes over him, warming him clean through. His brain is seriously muddled, but he doesn't think it's from the hangover.

"I'm from Connecticut," she says. "Why did you think Kansas?"

Her hazel eyes gaze steadily on him, waking him from his stupor. He resists the urge to blush when he's caught staring.

His hands wave around a little as he answers. "I don't know, I guess it was your skirt. It reminds me of the prairie," he offers as his voice trails off.

She jams her hands in her sweater pockets as she stands in front of him. "Boy, you and Charmaine really don't like my long skirts," she mutters.

"They just make you look shorter," he comments, and her eyes widen in surprise.

"Do you have a filter, or?" she demands.

He leans back on the couch. "I'm just saying they're not very flattering for your build."

Jeri gasps. Her hand flies to her chest as if she's in pain before leveling him with a glare. "Why does it matter how I dress? Do you think it affects my ability to do my job?"

He shrugs. "I guess it's fine for work, but why would you wear it to a bar?"

Her stare doesn't let up. "Maybe I was protesting the archaic idea of getting all dolled up and inebriated in order to find the opposite sex attractive," she declares.

Caden feels a little bad about being so personal, but she went after him first. Try as he might, he can't regret getting her fired up. Her cheeks are pink. Her fists are clenched. Tension rolls off her. He's more interested in her than he's been in anyone in a long time. The realization sits in his stomach like a rock.

"I never said anythin' about your ability to do your job," he grounds out. "I could say somethin' about you actin' like an overly zealous church lady who is one step away from being a member of the red hat club, but that would be *of-fensive*," he bellows.

Her jaw drops. Her face flames. She looks like she's about

to cry. He feels terrible. She ducks her head. Her shoulders shake. He can't believe what's happening or that he made her breakdown in tears. He's not sure what to do. He's two giant steps away from offering an extremely awkward hug when the sound of laughter permeates the room. She holds her stomach while she stomps her foot, doing some strange sort of dance. He breathes a sigh of relief. A satisfied smirk pops out of him.

He taps an impatient finger on his knee as he waits for her to quiet down so they can visit. "What are you doin' here?" he asks.

Jeri opens her mouth to answer and then closes it. She has no explanation because she's not too sure herself. "I already told you. I was giving you a ride home."

"But you live in the city, which is like almost an hour from here," he states.

"*I know that.* I just drove over from the office," she grinds out.

He studies her a little too long. Jeri supposes she should feel offended, but there's nothing pervy about his observations, more like curiosity. "Do you drive an hour out of your way to pick up all your clients?" he says in a flirty tone.

Jeri knows he's fishing for information she doesn't want to give, but he's also just being a shameless flirt. It's a legitimate question, but she's pretty sure he already knows the answer. He just wants to see her squirm. "It depends on the circumstance," she responds.

"Mmm hmmm. And do you always walk *inmates* to their front doors?" he continues. She feels like he just put her on the defense, and she's not sure how she feels about it. The man is way too comfortable in his own skin. That has to be what the attraction is. *Stop it, Jeri. Do not think about that word again.*

"I need to use the restroom," she blurts out. "I don't like to use the ones at the facility."

He gestures to somewhere behind him. "Go ahead. It's right down that hall," he says in a daring voice.

His voice tells her he doesn't believe a word she's saying as she scurries past him, beating a hasty retreat from Mr. Smug Pants. Boy, does he wear those pants well.

Jeri turns on the cold water and splashes herself in the face a few times. "Girl, get a grip," she whispers. "This isn't high school. You're a grown woman. Do your job," she scolds before drying her face and walking back out to find him sitting where she left him. She clears her throat. "Guess I'll be going then. I'm not surprised to see you again. I told you where you'd end up," she taunts. She can't believe her need to keep him at a distance causes her to be so rude.

He knows she's attracted, just like he knows she's determined to ignore it. Her all-knowing declaration pushes his last button. "I bet you paid him to start a fight with me. That's probably what you were doin' at the bar in the first place, ensurin' job security," he accuses, even though he feels way too close to being some sort of crazy conspiracy theory guy who hoards newspapers and padlocks his own fridge.

She stops her walk toward his front door. She spins around. There's fire in her eye. She's so hot.

"What did you just say?" she spits at him.

"You heard me," he growls.

"Do you *honestly think* I paid a stranger to help you make a complete ass of yourself? It's clear you don't need any of my help in that department."

Caden couldn't agree with her more, but he's not about

to admit it. "I think it's about time you left, darlin'. You've overstayed your welcome, and I'm about to get *real* comfortable," he says as he touches the top button of his jeans.

Her face flushes. She averts her eyes. He feels like a pig, but he's not about to take his hand off his top button.

"I'm sure we'll be in touch soon," she chokes out. She almost trips over her feet while backing up.

He can't believe what a jerk he's being. He tries to lighten the uncomfortable mood he created. "Jeri," he says in a soft voice as if she's a skittish horse. "I'm sorry if I read you all wrong. It's just...you didn't need to come inside to tell me any of this," he explains in the most unoffensive tone he's ever used. He can't believe he's pulling out all the stops on his bond lady. "I thought you were interested on a more personal level," he says in a half-wounded manner. He can't believe what a wuss he's being.

Jeri wishes he'd take his hand off the button of his pants. She can't believe he was acting like he was going to start stripping right in front of her just to make her blush. Now he's acting all apologetic and using some wimpy voice she's sure he didn't know he had. Even so, she's appalled to find herself a little weak in the knees at his attempts to be less of the pig he was being just seconds ago. He's so confusing. The worst part is she finds herself strongly attracted to her client, which is definitely a first and something she never thought would happen.

She clears her throat. "I assure you I am here in a strictly professional capacity," she states in her gritchiest tone, but he keeps right on smiling. She fights the urge to smile back. "I'm going to go now," she says as she turns and heads for his front door.

Caden watches her leave. He's overcome with the sudden

urge to feel her touch. He has to know if the electricity between them that night at the bar was a fluke. He jumps up off the couch and strides across the room. "I apologize. Where are my manners?" he asks as he sticks out his hand.

Jeri stands with one hand on the doorknob while she stares at his outstretched hand as if it's a snake or something that's about to bite her. Her mouth feels as dry as cotton. She drops her hand from the doorknob and takes a few small steps in his direction before placing her small hand in his big one. His hand is warm as it swallows hers up. She doesn't know what to say, and so she gives it a quick squeeze. It's harder than she intended, but the jolt of electricity shooting up her arm is so unexpected.

Caden chokes a little. He drops his hand. His face colors. He stares down at her. "Thank you for bailin' me out and drivin' me home even though I'm a *grown man,*" he says with a smirk. "It is your job after all," he says with a knowing wink that tells her he must have bat ears, because she's certain he heard her whispering to herself in his bathroom.

Jeri holds his stare as she looks up at him, but it's hard. She's positively mortified. "You're welcome," she manages before she whirls around so fast her skirt fills with air. It swirls around before settling against her as she walks out. Her heart races as she hurries down the sidewalk, admonishing herself all the way. "Get a grip, Jeri. He's just a man," she mutters beneath her breath, "whose number you don't have," she continues and resists the urge to turn around and march right back in there. She climbs into her car and starts it up. "I have his address, so I'll just mail him his court date," she reasons as she pulls away from his curb and slowly re-enters traffic.

Caden reels from the touch of her hand, just like he did

that night at the bar. He plops down on the couch and runs his hands through his hair, grinning. "A bail bondsman. I'll be danged," he mutters as he shakes his head back and forth. "A bail bondswoman," he repeats as he lays a hand across his chest.

four

Jeri's head swims with thoughts of Caden all the way back to the office. She's barely in the door when Charmaine spots her. "There you are. I thought you'd gone missing. I was ready to call out an APB on you," she says with a serious look on her face. "You've been gone for like at least two hours."

Jeri rolls her eyes. "Whatever. I picked up a guy. He lives out of town," she says about the time she catches the excitement in her tone, but she can't take it back. By the look on Charmaine's face, she heard it too.

"A new guy, huh. Is he cute?"

Jeri grins before she can stop herself. She knows she should just tell Charmaine who he is, but she decides to drag it out as long as possible. Charmaine never tires of hearing a good story, and for reasons Jeri's not ready to admit, she's in the mood to tell a whopper. "It doesn't matter what he looks like, but yes, he is not unfortunate looking."

Charmaine grins even bigger. "Is he married? Does he have a serious significant other, or..."

Jeri frowns at her. "I don't know. I didn't see any pictures in frames at his apartment," she says absent-mindedly as she searches her mind for evidence of a woman in his life.

Charmaine's brown eyes bug. "You went in his place? How did that happen?"

Jeri throws her hands up in the air. "Sometimes we go to their homes. What's the big deal?" she says as she flops down in her chair and grins.

Charmaine leans back in her office chair and stares Jeri down with her arms crossed beneath her chest and her lower lip sticking out. "Hmm mmm. *I* go out to people's houses as much as I can because I get bored. *You* practically live here. If I didn't know better, I'd say you were *chained* to your desk," she continues. "He must be somethin' special if you made a *house call.*" Charmaine says in a way that makes it sound a little dirty, like only Charmaine can do.

"Maybe I decided to venture out a little," Jeri argues, but it's weak.

"Or maybe you met a hot guy, and he piqued your interest," Charmaine fires right back while keeping a close eye on Jeri to gage her reaction to her accusation. Jeri sits down at her desk. She fiddles with her papers beneath Charmaine's direct stare. "You know I ain't gettin' nothin' done until you finish the story," Charmaine taunts.

Jeri gives her an ornery look. "I never started the story."

Charmaine raises an eyebrow in warning. "Then start it already. I'm gettin' old over here."

Jeri exhales slowly. "The whole thing is hinky anyway."

Charmaine giggles. "Hinky? That's a fun word." She stares Jeri down. "Go on then. What happened next?"

Jeri gives her a direct look. "Are you going to let me tell it?"

Charmaine does a huge eye roll. "Yeah, girl. Get to tellin'."

Jeri sits up straighter in her chair. Her excitement builds as soon as she thinks about seeing Caden again. She doesn't want it to stop. "So I was in here all alone, minding my own business, and Miles walked in."

Charmaine slaps the desk hard enough to startle her. "Girl, tell me it's not Miles that's got you all flighty and cute. The man's a lyin' cheat. You done caught the boy red-handed."

Jeri puts up one hand. Charmaine stops talking. Jeri takes a deep breath. "As I was saying, Miles walks in here with no warning. He hands me a thousand-dollar check and tells me he's got a guy he owes a favor to, and he doesn't want it hanging over his head," Charmaine clears her throat and stares even harder at Jeri who pauses, "I know. Miles is still a jerk. So, anyway, Miles gives me this money and tells me he's got a friend who's in jail downtown because he got in a fight last Friday night down at the bar, but his friend is too stubborn to call someone to get him out. Miles said his friend had to be released, or he would lose his job."

Charmaine taps her nails on the desk. "So what did you do?"

Jeri wiggles in her seat. "Well, a thousand dollars is a thousand dollars, so I took the check and went to the next town over and bailed the guy out, and that's it," she says and waits for a response.

"That doesn't tell me how you got to be in the guy's place," Charmaine prompts.

Jeri tries to sit still, but she can't stop fidgeting under Charmaine's prying eyes. "Oh, yeah. So I offered him a ride home because his car wasn't there because the cops took him down there Saturday morning."

Charmaine makes a face at Jeri. "Gee, Jeri. How *neighborly* of you. That's not like you at all. You *never* give men rides from the jail, and you *never* go inside strange men's apartments. You're as paranoid as a gun-loving NRA nut, so what's so special about this guy?"

Jeri stills and stares at her computer screen, but she's not really seeing it. "I don't know, but there's just something about him," she says in a quiet voice.

"What's he look like?"

"He's a little over six foot. He has dark brown wavy hair. His build almost looks slight, but it's not. He's kind of immovable, but in a good way. I've seen a lot of brown eyes, but there's just something about his that make them special." She pauses. "Maybe it's the way he looks at me. It's so sincere. There's like, no hidden motives. I guess I'm not used to a guy being so straight forward. It might sound cheesy, but he's a good, solid, guy," Jeri answers.

Charmaine fakes a snore. "Girl. That sounds like a whole lotta boring." She snaps her fingers. "Kinda like that guy we met the other night, the one who was into you, even though you were too busy rippin' him a new one to even notice he was kinda ho-ot," Charmaine says with a pout. Jeri can't believe Charmaine is still upset about not havin' a drink with Caden.

"The guy's not too boring. He was in jail after all," Jeri teases her co-worker before she turns serious and frowning. "That's not really funny. I shouldn't have said that."

Charmaine giggles. "It's a little funny. What'd you say his name is?"

"You don't need his name to know who he is," Jeri teases.

Charmaine looks all sorts of confused. "Why's that?"

Jeri leans forward in her chair. She rests her elbows on her knees and tilts her head a little sideways until her bun sort of flops. "He's not *kind of* like the guy at the bar. He *is* the guy from the bar," Jeri answers, with a self-satisfied grin.

Charmaine's jaw drops. "No friggin' way," she says in a voice filled with awe.

Jeri is used to Charmaine's outrageous antics, but she still gets a kick out of them every time she witnesses her friend's expressions. "Yes friggin' way," she answers right back. "I totally called it," she practically sings.

Charmaine laughs out loud. "You so did," she crows but then stops. "Wait, what? What did you call?"

Jeri rolls her eyes. "I told him that night, Charmaine. I told him he'd end up in a jail cell, and he did."

Charmaine waves her hand in the air. "I met him. He's not a criminal. I'm sure he had a good reason."

Jeri agrees, but she's not about to admit it. "You're just sayin' that because he's hot," she argues.

"Ha, I knew you thought he was hot," Charmaine sings at her friend.

Jeri eyeballs Charmaine. "His name is Caden. He's not that hot," she states, as if saying the words aloud will make her immune to his touch and the coy looks he gave her, setting off butterflies. She says no more as she tries to ignore Charmaine and push any thought of Caden and his hotness from her brain.

She gets to work on the stack of papers that haven't moved an inch since she walked out the door with Miles. The rest of the day flies by. Her head hurts from all the measly excuses she's heard from half her clients about why they can't show up to court for their first appearance in front of the judge, no matter how many times and different ways Jeri explains to them what will happen if they don't. For the life of her, Jeri cannot figure out why people expect a judge to operate on their time.

She locks the front door as she and Charmaine walk out together. A pale piece of paper is stuck beneath her windshield wiper. Thoughts of Ben Stine assail Jeri. She glances around to see if anyone is in the area. Ben was harmless enough as a person and a client, but he took pulling pranks to a whole new level. It started with a simple parking ticket that he found on his car downtown. The meter man was just doing his job, handing out tickets to people who didn't feed their meters, but to Ben, it was as if the city had thrown their sword onto his side of the imaginary battlefield. Things escalated quickly between Ben and the city.

He routinely stole tablets of blank tickets off the meter man's golf-cart-like transportation. Ben slathered Vaseline all over the meter man's steering wheel, seat, and mirrors. Although those actions were irritating and a hassle, they weren't technically anything to get Ben thrown in jail. The thing that got Ben in the worst trouble was when he started writing his own tickets on the stolen tablets and leaving them on city worker's vehicles. Once he met Jeri, he would leave one for her too, but hers were dinner invitations.

Jeri reaches for the paper-thin carbon-copy piece of paper stuck beneath her wiper. She opens it out of curiosity and a little fear. She heard Ben moved back to his hometown, which means he shouldn't be anywhere near. '415-232-7511' is scrawled in messy handwriting across the piece of paper. At least she thinks that's what it says. She's not sure of all the numbers. The person's handwriting is atrocious. Charmaine snatches the paper from her hand. "Girl, did you get a note?"

Jeri stares at it some more, but it's hard to see all of it when Charmaine's coffin nails are covering the important parts of the note. She jabs a fingernail at letters covering the corner.

"Ooh. C.B., that stands for Caden Brown. He gave you his digits." She turns to Jeri with a big grin. "That means he's interested." Charmaine's brown eyes sparkle and shine. She claps her hands and bounces on her tiptoes, making the rest of her bounce too.

Jeri lays a hand on her co-workers arm. "Charmaine. Calm down. You're gonna bounce right out of your bra." She takes the paper back, folds it carefully in half and sticks it in her sweater pocket. "I'm not so sure that's him. I can't even read his writing."

Despite Jeri's negativity, Charmaine's smile doesn't diminish even a little. "It's him, Jeri. I know it is." She cocks her head to the side. "You about to have a boyfriend," she sings.

Jeri rolls her eyes at her co-workers' junior-high-like antics. "Get a grip, Charmaine. He is my client. To date him would be unprofessional," she states, even as her hand keeps a hold of the folded-up piece of paper in her pocket. "If it is his number, he just gave it to me because I didn't get it from him earlier." She drags her boot across the parking lot cement. "I was just going to mail his court date to his address."

Charmaine wiggles her eyebrows. "Well. Now you don't have to, you can call him instead."

Jeri's phone vibrates. Charmaine squeals. "Is it him?"

Jeri glances at her screen. "No. It's Miles."

Charmaine wrinkles her nose. "Ewww."

Jeri smiles at her friend. "I know," she says as she scans his text.

MILES:

Did you get him out of jail? What did he say? Are we even now?

Jeri starts to text him back but stops because she feels Charmaine's eyes boring into her. She looks up from her phone. "He wants to know if I picked him up, what he said, and if they're even. Apparently, Miles owed Caden a favor, and so that's why he bonded him out."

Charmaine nods her head. "Yeah, you told me already."

Jeri holds up her phone. "Oh. Sorry." She shakes her head. "Miles has texted me back quicker today than he ever did when we were together." She frowns. "Go figure."

Charmaine kicks a rock across the lot. "It's good you found out about Miles early so you could dump him. You don't need a liar and a cheat. No one does. You're smarter and stronger now. You're ready for a real relationship with a real guy, like this Caden Brown dude. I've got a good feelin' about him," she says with a smile.

Jeri holds her tongue. It wouldn't be helpful to tell Charmaine she says that about every guy she thinks Jeri ought to date. It's not her friend's fault she's so particular. "Thanks, Charmaine," she says instead. "See you tomorrow," she adds before getting back to answering Miles.

JERI:

He's back home. He doesn't know why you bonded him out. He says you didn't owe him anything, and he told you that.

49

She climbs into her Lemonade Spark car and heads for the gym. Her phone goes off again. She answers through her steering wheel. "Hey, girl. My friends and I are going out tonight, do you wanna come?" Charmaine's friendly invitation tempts Jeri until she remembers the last time she went out with Charmaine and her friends. Jeri got fall-down drunk off a bunch of shots, puked them all up in an alley, and then had a hangover that lasted the last half of the work week.

"Um, no thanks. I'm going to the gym on my way home. I've got a couple of frozen pizzas and some veggies I gotta eat before they go bad," she adds.

"Snore, Jeri. Your life is so predictable," Charmaine whines in her ear.

"I know, and I like it that way, Char. Go on and have your fun with your friends. I'll talk to you tomorrow."

"Are you sure? I'm going out with the fab four," Char sings/shouts.

Jeri backs away from her voice that booms from the steering wheel out of instinct. "Haven't three of the fab four been your clients?" Jeri asks.

"They aren't anymore, so it's fine," Charmaine reassures her. "I gotta go," she says in a slightly less friendly tone.

"Bye," Jeri says.

"Byeeee," Charmaine responds, and then there's silence on the line.

Jeri pulls into the gym parking lot on the edge of the city. It takes her almost half an hour to get there, but the drive is a good wind-down after a long day at work. She parks beside an older-looking motorcycle. She can't help but notice her tiny car is about as short as the bike. She wrinkles her nose as she walks by it. "I hate bikes," she grumps.

She scans her gym pass at the door and walks inside

before heading straight for the locker room. Jeri changes out of her work clothes into a pair of yoga pants, tee shirt, and lightweight sweatshirt. She tugs on her ankle socks and tennis shoes. She wanders over to the yoga mats, grabs one up and goes to the far side of the room to sit and stretch. She has her earbuds in so she doesn't have to make small talk with anyone. After ten minutes of stretching, she takes the yoga mat back and hops on the elliptical. She cranks her music and goes hard for the next half hour. It feels good to shut everything and everyone out for a little while. She hops off the elliptical and heads for the equipment side.

Jeri does some arm and leg work. She has a strange feeling that someone might be watching her, but she's not about to look around. It always feels like she's staring at someone or interrupting their workout. Jeri treats the gym like work. She goes in, makes the most of her time, and then goes home to relax. She's in the middle of her last leg exercise on the sled when something brushes the side of her face and pops out her earbud. She jerks her head to the side, letting the sled fall a little too fast. It's jarring. A noisy breath escapes her. "I said, did you get my number?" a familiar voice asks in her ear.

Jeri turns to face him. He's so close her forehead almost hits his chin. She backs away a bit and finds herself staring into Caden's beautiful brown eyes and friendly smile. "I did," she answers back in a tone much louder than his, because she's talking over the earbud in her other ear. She climbs out of the sled machine awkwardly. He shows no interest in backing up to give her some space. She shoos at him with her hands. "You could have just come in the office and seen me," she adds.

He looks all sheepish. "I didn't want to go inside your building," he says with his voice lowered.

"Because you didn't want to be seen walking into my office," she booms at a volume Caden didn't know she was capable of.

"Something like that, yeah," he replies.

Jeri understands what he's saying, but it's her job, and she's feeling defensive. "I'll have you know I've served some pretty well-known people," she argues, even though she feels ridiculous doing it. "Everyone gets in a pinch now and then," she adds to try and soften the blow.

Caden's finger is on his lips, trying to shush her as he stares at her with widened eyes. "Anyway, you have my number, so feel free to call me if you need anything," he says with a confidence and swagger that puts the blush back in Jeri's cheeks. She feels like people are staring at the two of them, and she doesn't like it.

She takes a few more steps back and stares him right in the eye with a look that she hopes conveys she's not the one who's desperate for a phone call. "Yeah, well. You've got my number too. I think you'll be the one calling me," she says and pauses for dramatic effect, "if you know what's good for you," she adds before spinning on her heel.

She goes to jam her earbud back in her ear and comes up empty-handed. She turns back around. Caden stands across the gym from her, holding her earbud in his hand with a flirty smirk, as if to say, *come and get it.* Something about him standing there holding her earbud hostage sends her over the edge of reason. She spins back around and stomps all the way to the girl's locker room, ignoring the amused looks of a few gym members who couldn't help but overhear their heated exchange.

Jeri kicks off her gym shoes and socks and slides her feet into her boots. She's so angry she doesn't care if she's wearing workout clothes with western-style boots. She strides straight out the front door and heads for her car. She's halfway down the sidewalk when she looks up to see Caden leaning on the bike. "It figures he would drive a motorcycle," she whispers beneath her breath like a madwoman. She marches over to her car without a word and opens the door. She tosses her gym bag in the passenger seat and hops in. She starts up her car while staring straight ahead. She's determined not to look at him.

five

Caden Brown watches Jeri with no small amount of humor. The lady can really get a bug up her butt, he thinks right before he remembers her butt in her yoga pants which he didn't want to do because it makes him feel a little like a perv. He focuses on the earbud in his hand and the fact that she's determined to ignore him. He hops on his motorcycle and follows her out of the parking lot.

"She saw my place, so I can see hers," he reasons so he doesn't feel like a stalker. "I was at the gym first. She followed me there," he continues as he stays close enough to let her know she's being followed, but not too close to get a ticket for tailgating.

Ten minutes later, she turns into the backlot of an apartment building a few blocks from the ghetto side of town. Caden stays on his bike and waits for her to get out of her car. He feels ridiculous, but there's something about getting off the bike that seems a bit too aggressive. She looks more than annoyed as she takes her sweet time getting out of her car. She takes a few steps toward him but stops more than an arm's length away. "Do you make a habit of tailing people all over town?" she demands.

He knows she doesn't mean to be funny, but he can't help but laugh at her question. "Do you make a habit of drivin' off with one earbud?"

A breeze blows, and a hair or two escapes her bun falling in her face. Her hand flies out with her palm open. "May I have it back please?"

He removes it from his ear, enjoying the way her eyes widen when she realizes he's been listening to her music all this time. "Your taste in music sucks," he comments and waits for her fiery temper. By the furious look on her face, he won't be disappointed.

Her hand flies to her hip. "If you don't like my music then don't listen to it," she fires back.

He shrugs his shoulders in a nonchalant manner that tells her the madder she gets, the calmer he will be. "I was drivin'. I needed both hands for my bike. Safety is my priority," he says with an ornery wink.

She shoves the earbud in her gym bag. "Are we done here? I've got things to do."

Caden doesn't care for her breezy dismissal of his presence, which must be the only reason he climbs off his bike and walks over to peek in her car window. He breathes easy when he sees her backseat full of boxes. "You need a hand with anything?" he asks.

Jeri hesitates before she makes a strange sound that he thinks implies surrender. "Fine. If you could carry those boxes for me, I'd really appreciate it," she says in a resigned tone seriously lacking enthusiasm that suggests he's a dentist getting ready to pull her tooth. He thinks she should be a little more grateful, but she didn't say no. Caden opens the back door to her tin can car and makes quick work of stacking the three boxes on the pavement before picking them all up at once. He is surprised to find out how dejected he is to see they appear to have cathouses in them. He hates cats. He was hoping he was wrong in his initial suspicion that Jeri is a cat person. Just because she dresses like a grandma at work doesn't necessarily mean she is destined to be a spinster with a bunch of cats to keep her company.

He keeps a close eye on the ground as he moseys across the lot. He doesn't want to trip over a parking curb. He pauses when he hears her clearing her throat. He peeks around his piled-up boxes resting against his chest and chin. Jeri stands at a door to the apartment building tapping her toe.

"I'm comin'," he says. "These boxes are awkward to carry, and I can't see where I'm goin'."

She rolls her eyes at him. "I never asked you to carry them, did I?"

Caden is one step away from setting them down on the sidewalk and leaving, but he wants to see her place, even though it makes no sense at all. He says nothing in response and keeps walking toward her while he watches his step. Jeri stands at the door as he walks by. She can't help but notice the faint smell of his cologne as he walks by, but there's something else too, something that she's certain is just part of who he is, something that makes her want to be near him. It's the same thing that makes her keep her distance.

Jeri lets the door close and starts to walk down the hallway and just about runs into him. "What are you doing?" she asks in alarm as she literally falls against the wall to avoid bumping into him.

He smirks at her as if he knows the effect he has on her.

This doesn't make her feel any better. "I'm waitin' for you to tell me where to go," he says.

She makes a big show of stepping clear around him, giving him plenty of space. Three doors later, she stops and knocks on the door.

"Do you always knock on your own door?" Caden teases.

Jeri turns sideways to face him. "This isn't my apartment," she says with an ornery grin. "It's my guy's."

His smile falters just a little, and Jeri notices. She feels a tiny bit bad. "I didn't know," he says, acting all flustered. "I wouldn't have followed you home from the gym," he protests.

"Over an earbud?" she questions in a teasing tone, and Caden feels slightly better. He's still embarrassed, but that's better than her thinking he's chasing after someone who is seeing someone else.

He sets the boxes down beside her. "Here. I'm just gonna go. I wouldn't want you to get in any trouble or whatever," he explains, feeling more awkward by the second.

"Hold your horses, girlie, I'm comin'" a gravelly voice booms from the other side of the door about the time Jeri looks caught. Caden stops in his tracks as he's backing away. He creeps up the hallway and leans against the far wall within sight of the door. There's a sliding of the chain and a turning of the doorknob. A tall, white-haired man in glasses stares out at them.

"Jeri, how nice to see you. I see you brought a friend," he booms as he waves wildly at the two of them. "Come in, come in. I was just making some tea," he says as he wraps a long arm around Jeri and gives her a squeeze. He looks over his shoulder and gives Caden a wink. "Come in, son, and bring those boxes with you."

Caden doesn't know what to think, but he's got nowhere to be, so he steps inside. "Uncle Saul, this is Caden," Jeri all but shouts.

The old man makes a show of sticking his finger in his ear and wiggling it a bit. "Tone it down a bit, Jeri. I've got my hearing aids in," he says before he goes to the sink and washes his hands and dries them on a kitchen towel before he walks back over to where Caden stands in the middle of the living room. Saul extends his wrinkled hand, "Hello, Caden. It's nice to meet ya. How do you know my Jeri?"

Caden catches the smirk on her face. He can't wait to erase it. "She tried to pick me up at a bar the other night," he answers.

Her smirk turns into a scowl. She walks into his space. "I most certainly did not," she says as she stares up at him.

He grins down at her with a teasing look on his face. "Yeah, you did. You gave me your number. What else would you call it?"

Jeri resists the ridiculous urge to stomp on his foot. She settles for poking him in the chest. "I gave you my business card because I was sure you would end up in jail," she accuses. Her face is so close to his he feels her hot breath on his chin. It drives him crazy. "And you did," she says with a wicked gleam in her hazel eyes.

Caden opens his mouth. He closes it again. He can't believe she outed him in front of her uncle, who studies him with an expression that's hard to read.

"Something tells me there's a little more to the story," Saul says, but he doesn't sound too upset about it.

Caden nods his head. "Um, yeah. She kind of had to bail me out," he admits. It's the first time he's felt embarrassed since the fight.

Saul tosses his head back and laughs. "Oh, boy. I knew it would be a doozy." He waves a hand at Caden. "You've got trouble written all over ya," he says as he slaps Caden on the back with strength that surprises him, "but it's the good kind, boy. It's the good kind," Saul says as he leans forward and looks him in the eye. "I got myself thrown in the clink once too, ya know, and I turned out alright."

Caden swallows hard. He's not sure how to answer, especially considering Jeri looks at the two of them like she'd like to dump 'em both in the middle of a river and let 'em swim back to shore. "Yeah, well, it's definitely not something I want to repeat," Caden answers, because he means it, and he doesn't know what else to say.

Saul squeezes his shoulder, and he's got a grip. "Good thing is you learned your lesson. That's what important," he growls.

Caden nods as he tries to wiggle out of Saul's firm grasp. "Yep, that's right."

Saul glances at him out of the corner of his eye. "What do you know about putting cathouses together?"

Caden breathes a little easier. He's ready to talk about something besides jail. "I know a little about tools and carpentry," he offers. "Are there instructions?" Saul gives him a funny look.

Caden coughs. "Who needs instructions? I think they're more of a suggestion anyways," he adds.

Saul laughs and claps his hands. "That's my boy." He looks over at Jeri. "Jeri, would you mind baking me some of your famous cookies that I love so much?"

Jeri scowls at her uncle and Caden. "You mean the kind that come straight out of a tube? Sure, I'll get right on that," she answers in a flat tone.

Saul ignores his niece's snarky comment. "Sounds great. Thanks Jeri." Saul looks in her direction again. "So, which idiot took the cake this week?"

Jeri gives her uncle a pointed look, glances at Caden, and then looks back at her uncle. "You know I can't talk shop in front of a client."

Saul nudges Caden in the ribs. "Since she can't tell me about her other clients, why don't you tell me what *you* did, and make it as interesting as possible."

Caden clears his throat and pretends Jeri isn't there, mostly, as he fills Saul in on the last night he was at the bar. "Well, I was in a small dive bar on the edge of the city Friday night."

Saul holds up a hand. "Which one?"

"No Minors," Caden answers.

Saul laughs a good long laugh. "That's pretty good." He pauses. "Is it new? I don't think I know it."

"It used to be Hippies and Hogs," Jeri states.

They both turn to look at her in question.

"What?" She says. "With all my clients you think I don't know every bar within a hundred-mile radius?" She holds up under her uncle's scrutiny. "Not that it's any of your business, but I don't go in them unless it's for work. Geez. Talk about a double standard," she mutters, but Saul has already turned away from his niece.

"Okay, what happened next?" Saul asks Caden with an expectant tone. Caden dumps the contents of the three boxes on the floor and starts sorting the screws. "You wanna know what happened *before or after* some bossy, uptight, little blonde shoved her card in my face and called me a criminal?" he asks while telling himself not to feel bad about being so critical of Jeri when everything he just said was the truth.

Saul laughs out loud. "That's my niece," he nods. "To a tee."

Jeri drops a pan on the countertop. Twice. "I can make blackened cookies, Uncle. They are my specialty," she threatens.

Saul turns toward the kitchen. "No, thank you," he says before turning back to Caden. "What happened after?"

Caden stops what he's doing and rests his hands on his thighs as he sits on his knees on the floor. "It all started when he sat on my favorite bar stool," he says in a manner worthy of the witness box in a courtroom.

Saul nods his head. "Aw, yes. He was spoilin' for a fight," he says in complete agreement.

Caden knows Bairn had no idea it was his stool, but Saul is so agreeable. He doesn't correct him. "So I'm sittin' two stools down, mindin' my own business, sippin' my Bud Light,"

"Cause you gotta watch your calories," Saul interjects. "Ladies don't want the Michelin Man," he says with a chuckle as he taps his own mostly flat stomach. "I eat an apple a day, walk four miles, do my push-ups and sit-ups," he nods. "It's important to stay active." Caden eyes the instructions laying on the floor with the numbered pieces on them. He picks the first one up and fits it to the next one, lining up the corresponding holes. He looks over at Saul, who looks back at him. "What happened next?" Saul asks.

Caden searches his brain for what he last said before he was interrupted. "Just a second. Can you hold these together please?"

Saul reaches for them but stops. "Hey, Jeri. Can you come hold something for us? My hands are too shaky," he says. Caden studies Saul's hands. They look pretty steady to him, but he keeps his mouth shut. If it takes an ornery old man to get Jeri sitting closer to him, he'll play along.

Jeri stands in the kitchen with her hand on her hip. "I'm baking cookies," she protests.

Saul turns to his niece. "Get in here, girl. It'll only take a few minutes."

Jeri raises an eyebrow as she walks across the room and plops down beside her uncle. "What am I doing?"

Saul gives her a playful shove, and she falls over sideways on her butt, bumping into Caden who keeps a hold of the cathouse pieces. Jeri clumsily gets back up, giving Caden a dirty look.

"Don't help me up or anything," she grumbles.

"I wouldn't dream of it," he replies in a dry tone. "I'm not the one who shoved you over," he says as he holds the pieces together. "I just need you to hold these together so I can put the screws in."

"Fine," she says as she scoots closer and grabs a hold of them. Caden leans over the pieces. There's too much shadow and not enough space. He sits back up.

"I need you to hold it differently," he says.

"How?" she demands in a testy tone of voice.

"In a way that I can see what I'm doin' and reach it without getting' a serious crick in my neck," he responds with a bit of impatience in his voice.

"Is that all?" she pops off as she slowly rotates the pieces while staring him down with fight in her eyes. It's hard, but he stops staring her in the eye and looks down.

"There," he says. "Hold it right there," he demands as he fits the screw in the hole and starts to turn the screwdriver. He applies more pressure as it tightens, and she can't hold it in place.

"Hold up, I need somethin' under it," she grumps. He stops turning the screw but doesn't move the screwdriver. She sets it against her leg, bumping up against him as he kneels over the wood.

"So I was sittin' there drinkin' my beer, and the guy on my favorite stool recognizes me because we went to school together," he continues with his story. "And so he starts jawin' like he always does whenever he runs into anyone from high school about when we played basketball and how great we were. Except we weren't, which is fine by me. But I guess he can't accept it. I don't know, so I'm sittin' there, tryin' to watch the game on the small flat screen TV in the corner of the bar that he's blockin' with his big head. He's talkin' so loud I can't hear the announcer on the TV, and I can't see the game, and my favorite team was playin'."

"Let me guess, the Wolverines," Jeri says in a dry tone.

Caden takes the pieces back from her and starts fitting another one to it before resituating it on her lap. "Hold it like this please, and yes, it was the Wolverines," he adds.

"Did they win?" Saul asks.

Caden shoots him a grin. "No. We were goin' back and forth until the last seven minutes of the game, which I missed because of Bairn and his stupid storytellin' and stupid fat head like I said. So when I saw my team lost and I missed the whole thing, and he was still yakkin', I told him to shut-up. We had some ugly words, and then I told him I was going to the men's room. I went to go by him, and he punched me in the back so I turned around and punched him in the face, and that's when he pressed charges."

"So he was embarrassed because you insulted him and knocked him out at the bar," Saul says, but there's no judgment.

"Pretty much, yeah," Caden agrees.

"You can't go around punching people just because they're stupid," Jeri accuses.

Saul snorts at his niece's scolding. "Apparently not," he shakes his head. "I tell you what, that's just sad. You punched him once. It should have been one and done. It's not like it was premeditated. It's not like you were carrying a weapon." He studies Caden for half a second. "How big was this guy?"

Caden coughs a little. "Why does size matter?" he argues, but he speaks in a quiet tone.

Saul chuckles. "So he's a little fella," he correctly assumes.

"Yeah, well. He has a big mouth," Caden assures him as he takes the half-put-together cathouse back again.

A timer goes off. "Oh, shoot. Those are my cookies," Jeri says as she hops up and runs to the other room to remove the first batch from the oven.

Saul leans in, talking quieter. "So, how far did the little man fly?" he says before he chuckles again.

"I can totally hear you, Uncle, and you shouldn't encourage violence," Jeri scolds from the kitchen.

Jeri drops the pan on the top of the stove with a clatter. "Crapballs. I burned them," she mutters. "I'm staying in here, so I don't burn anymore," she complains as she glances at her watch. "It's 8 PM, Uncle Saul. Did you take your night-time meds?"

He dismisses her with a backwards wave. "I'll take them in a few minutes."

She gets in his cabinet, takes down his med minder, and pours them in a paper cup. She fills up a cup of water and takes both to her uncle, holding them out. "Here. Take them so I don't worry. Please."

Caden keeps his head down, not wanting to witness Saul's small surrender to his niece. The timer goes off again. Jeri runs in the kitchen and removes a second pan of cookies. They're not quite as burnt, but they're not great. She puts her last pan in, determined to keep a closer eye on them, but Caden is more of a distraction than she anticipated. She's never brought a guy around her uncle's apartment. Even though Caden followed her here uninvited, she knows the significance of his meeting her uncle, something she could have prevented if she really wanted to.

She gets stuck on that fact. She's only known Caden all of two days, and he's already wormed his way into her life. She has an uneasy feeling that all of this means a great more to her than to him. He's kind of hard to read. She thinks there's interest there on his part, but he's a client. She's never come close to crossing that line. Up until now, she's never wanted to.

The buzzer goes off, interrupting her unwelcome musings. She gets up from the table where she leans against the wall and out of sight of Caden and Saul, but that doesn't keep their voices from floating into the room with her. She turns off the oven, removes the tray of cookies from the stove, and places it on top.

She glances once more in Caden's direction. He sits in the Saul's rocker, laughing at something her uncle said. The cathouse sits in the middle of the floor, perfectly constructed. Caden catches her eye across the room. For half a second his laughter stops. He gives her a secret smile, and Jeri feels warm all over. Panic fills her. She has to leave. Now.

She snatches up her keys and walks through the living room on the way to the door.

"I just remembered I've got something in my car," she says before she opens the door and runs down the hallway. She feels ridiculous as she tries to outrun her feelings for Caden, but she's desperate. She's falling too hard and too fast, and they haven't even gone on a date. He's her client. She hops in her car and backs out of the lot as quiet as she used to coast into her parent's driveway in high school on the few nights she was out past her curfew.

Caden turns to Saul. "She took off on me, didn't she," he states more than asks.

Saul reaches over and pats his knee. "Give her some time, son. She'll come around." Saul wanders into his kitchen. "She wouldn't be afraid of something that's not there," he encourages. He holds up a cookie. "How do you feel about burnt cookies?"

Caden chuckles. "Do you have some milk to dip 'em in?"

Saul nods. "I do." He gives Caden a long look. "Do you play cards boy?"

Caden plops down in a kitchen chair. "I do."

Saul sets down two glasses of milk and a plate of cookies. "Well, alright. Let me go get those cards."

six

Jeri drives halfway across town to her tiny two-bedroom house, but she doesn't mind the size. It has the perfect front porch with a sidewalk leading up to it. She has just enough backyard for her two Frenchies, Butch Cassidy and the Sundance Kid, two reasons she bought a Chevy Spark instead of an Acadia. She wouldn't have it any other way. A white-picket fence encloses her picture-perfect house. She doesn't care how cheesy that makes her. She works hard for what she has.

Her phone buzzes on the kitchen countertop. She picks it up.

CADEN:

If I didn't know better, I'd say you're playin' hard to get.

She blushes all over again at his flirting.

JERI:

How'd you get my number?

CADEN:

I've had your number from the second we met. You're the one who gave it to me.

JERI:

Whatever. Next time you see Miles tell him he owes me ten grand if you don't show up to court.

CADEN:

Ten grand? Is that all I'm worth? When is the court date? Will you be there?

JERI:

I'll let you know the court date ASAP. If I'm there, it's for the money. Don't flatter yourself.

CADEN:

Gotta go. Your Uncle Saul is a shameless card shark. He's stealing all my burnt cookies.

Jeri lays her phone down with a smile. Her head is in the clouds. She can't believe he's playing cards with her uncle. "That is just the sweetest..." She stops talking and opens the fridge to figure out which leftover she's having for supper.

Her phone goes off again. It's a SnapChat from Charmaine who's sucking down a mixed drink from a big cup. There's only about a fourth of it left. "Hey, girll," she texts across the bottom.

Jeri snaps a pic of her blank fridge door. "Don't call me at midnight or later. I am not your DD." She types across the middle of the screen before hitting Send. Her Frenchies run circles around her ankles. She leans down to pet them before walking out the back door to the yard. Jeri walks the fence line while they chase each other around in the grass.

"I've never dated a client before. I don't think I can do it, but it doesn't matter because he didn't ask me out, so this is a stupid thing to get anxious about," she mumbles to the dogs as she walks in a bit of a rectangle.

Her phone goes off in her hand.

MOM

How was your day?

Jeri smiles.

JERI:

It was alright.

MOM:

Highlight?

JERI:

Saw Uncle Saul.

MOM:

How was he?

JERI:

Quite taken with Caden

She types and then erases it, because she knows once she hits Send, it will open a can of worms. Her mother will scold her for taking a client to see Uncle Saul. She won't understand why Jeri ran out of the gym with one earbud, practically inviting Caden to follow her to give it back, which only makes sense, because Jeri doesn't understand it either. Just like she doesn't understand the secret thrill she had over him chasing her on his motorcycle even though she acted like he was an idiot for doing so.

But if Jeri doesn't tell her mom about Caden, she feels like she is lying.

JERI:

He was happy to see me.

MOM:

Of course he was! Why wouldn't he be?

JERI:

I don't know.

"Because you aren't happy to see me unless I have a boyfriend," she mutters at her mother who lives three states away, but sometimes it still feels too close.

MOM:

My day was super exciting. Thanks for asking.

JERI:

I'm sorry. I was answering your last question. I didn't have time to say more than that.

MOM:

I went to the grocery store. They increased the price of beans by fifteen cents. Can you believe it? Your father was incensed!

JERI:

No. I can't believe it.

MOM:

I see you're as dry as milk toast. You know that's not how you catch a man.

JERI:

Maybe I'm not trying to.

MOM:

You can't have a family without a husband, Jeri. Don't you want children someday?

The thought of having children scares Jeri half to death. She can barely take care of herself, but when she thinks of the future, she sees little wavy-haired boys with ornery grins, much like Caden's. Jeri blinks. Her heart races. What was that about? It's all her mother's fault for asking such strange questions.

JERI:

It's getting late. I have a full day of work tomorrow. I really should go to sleep soon.

MOM:

Ah, yes. Another day of bailing criminals out of jail so they can roam the streets and commit more crimes. It's a good thing I'm not a worrywart.

JERI:

Yes, Mother. It truly is. Goodnight. I love you.

MOM:

I love you too. I really wish you'd meet someone.

JERI:

I met someone. His name is Caden. I picked him up from the jail and took him home. I even went inside his place.

MOM:

That's not funny, Jeri.

Jeri clutches her phone. "I know," she whispers because she doesn't disagree. Nothing about how she feels about Caden is funny, and she has no idea what to do about it.

JERI:

It's a little funny.

Jeri thinks of Caden's place, and she finds herself shopping online for University of Michigan sportswear. Her eyes light up when she finds an adorable hoodie.

"I can be supportive of the state I live in," she says to her Frenchies who look up at her while they wait for their expected daily treat. She orders the hoodie and the matching coffee cup and magnet. "What?" she says as she looks into their accusing faces. "I've been good. I haven't shopped online since I bought the over-sized snugli that just about took down my washer because it tried to squeeze the life out of my rotator thingie."

Jeri sits beside her Frenchies watching one of her favorite rom-coms, *Sleepless in Seattle*. She rubs her dogs' ears with one hand on each demanding head, knowing if she stops petting one but not the other, she won't hear anything but their whining. Jeri stares longingly at the screen.

"They just don't make 'em like Tom Hanks. There's the type of guy you fly halfway across the country for. I haven't met a guy I'd drive across town for," she mutters, right before images of Caden talking and laughing with her Uncle Saul pop into her head.

"So what if he gets along with my uncle who can be as cantankerous and painful as a canker sore. It's just because Caden is as difficult as he is," she grumbles. She lies back against the couch and puts her hands in her lap. Butch Cassidy and The Sundance Kid lay their heads in her lap, nudging her fingers with their wet noses.

Jeri returns to giving the tops of their heads a good scratching. "I need a Jonah to plan my love life for me," she says to her TV, "or at least give me a reason to have an adventure," she continues. Her phone vibrates. An e-mail pops up about six hours too late. "Seriously, Judge? You can't even give him more than a day's notice?" she gripes as she reads the e-mail. "If I keep texting him, he's going to think I'm flirting with him," she mutters while trying to ignore the way her heart feels like it's beating harder than usual. She stares at the black phone screen. "This is just stupid. It's work. It's not a date, which wouldn't happen because I don't ask guys out. They ask me out," she reaffirms as she types in Caden's number.

JERI:

Caden?

CADEN:

Yes.

JERI:

You have your first appearance tomorrow.
It's at 9:45.

CADEN:

What if I can't make it?

JERI:

You don't tell a judge you can't make it.

CADEN:

You didn't give me much notice.

JERI:

I told you as soon as I knew.

CADEN:

You sure about that? Is this just another
weak excuse to text me?

JERI:

Stop kidding around. This is me notifying
you that your first appearance is tomorrow.
Meet me tomorrow outside courtroom D on
the second floor. It's at Fourth and
Mechanic. Don't be late.

CADEN:

I'll give it my best shot.

JERI:

You'd better be there. I don't think you
want to have to pay nine-thousand dollars.

CADEN:

Why do I have to pay if I can't show up on
less than a days' notice?

JERI:

Just be there.

CADEN:

Yes ma'am.

Jeri blushes at his teasing. She turns her phone over. "Thanks a lot, Judge. I didn't need reminding the only interaction I'll have with a halfway decent guy who looks way too good in faded Levi's is off-limits," she mutters as she snaps her fingers. "That's what it is. He's a bad boy, and I've never dated a bad boy. That's all this is," she says, feeling better. "I just have to wait him out. It won't be long, and I won't have to see him anymore. It's going to be fine," she tells Butch Cassidy who looks at her with dark eyes full of doubt. Jeri hops off the couch. "Give me a break, Butch. It's been a while since I met a solid guy," she argues with herself, feeling more than a little crazy.

seven

Caden types himself a note on his phone. "Meet Jeri at the courthouse at 9:30 tomorrow," he mouths as he saves it. He plugs his phone into the wall and heads down the hall that leads to his bathroom to brush his teeth. He glances at the mirror.

"Time to face the music," he growls before spitting toothpaste into the sink. "Stupid Bairn. He's such a wuss," he mumbles before stalking out of the bathroom and down the hall to his room to try to get some sleep.

Morning comes too soon. Caden turns off the alarm clock too many times before getting out of bed. "Shoot. I'm going to be late to work," he says as he hurries around looking for the least wrinkled shirt that goes with his dark green tie and tan khakis. He knows he's dressing up a little more than usual, but it's important. He wants to make a good impression on the Judge, and if he's honest, Jeri, who seems just as determined to mostly ignore him as much as he wants her attention. Caden buttons up his shirt and shoves his feet into his favorite pair of dress shoes, ones that make him feel like a man's man, even though he knows the idea is absurd. They're just shoes.

The front door slams behind him. He turns to check the lock one more time before tossing on his helmet and hopping on his bike with his messenger bag tucked beneath his right elbow against his side.

Caden's phone vibrates nonstop in his inside jacket pocket the last three minutes of his drive to work. He checks it as soon as he pulls into the parking lot. It's Rafael, his right-hand man. It must be bad, or he wouldn't be calling, as Rafael is more than capable of handling whatever comes up beneath the ground. He listens to his voicemail. "We had a spill over between five and six AM best we can tell. I've spent the last few hours making sure all my men got out safely."

Caden's chest tightens a little less when he hears the men are all okay. He calls him back. "Hey, it's Caden. What happened?" he asks, trying not to sound accusatory, but he's alarmed.

"We're pretty sure it was an outside source, kind of like what happened at Lake Peigneur," he answers. "Whoever was on that job didn't pay any attention to our maps or markers," Rafael reports.

"Shit," Caden mutters. "My day is shot."

Rafael laughs in the phone. "Tell me about it."

Caden sighs heavily. His day in court is all but forgotten. "Hold up. I gotta call Judge Parker about something before I forget," Caden says. "Meet you at the site ASAP."

"Sounds good. Later," Rafael says right before Caden ends the call.

Caden scrolls through his contact list until he sees Judge Parker's name. He hits the call button. "Hey, Judge—"

"Hey, Carl," Judge Parker interrupts.

Caden clears his throat. "It's not Carl. It's Caden."

"You sound just like your old man, son. I thought you were calling to cancel on our golf game later this week."

Caden laughs. "Um, no. Actually, I don't know if you've noticed yet, but I'm scheduled to come in today. I got in a fight at the bar the other night, and the guy pressed charges."

The judge is silent for a few long seconds. "I see. Was it anyone I know?"

Caden blushes at the thought. "Probably. It was Bairn," he says in an embarrassed voice.

"Bairn as in baby-faced Bairn, your point guard from your basketball days who's like five feet tall?" the judge exclaims.

"Yeah," Caden replies.

"You've got a good foot on the guy," the judge barks.

"I know it. He sucker-punched me in the back," Caden protests.

"Okay," the judge says, but he doesn't sound convinced.

"The Wolverines lost a big game. I missed the last seven minutes because he wouldn't shut up."

"Aha. Now I get it," the Judge agrees, and Caden can't believe he forgot how big of a Wolverines fan the Judge is; so much so that he attends the games in an old bus he bought then had painted in Wolverines colors.

"So a lady named Jeri bailed me out and took me home, and I was supposed to appear before you today, but I had something come up at work. There's an emergency at the mine, and I'm very sorry, but I can't make it in this morning," Caden explains.

"No problem, son. I hear ya. You've got to take care of business," the Judge offers.

"Exactly. Thanks, Judge." Caden says. "I'm sorry, but I gotta get over there to the site."

"Sounds good. I'll talk to you soon enough," the Judge answers before he hangs up.

Forty minutes later, Jeri walks into an empty courtroom. To say she's surprised is an understatement. She walks down the long staircase and into the clerk of the district court's office. "Where's the Judge?" she asks.

"Excuse me?" the lady asks from behind her desk.

"I said where is the Judge?" Jeri demands.

"He's out 'til this afternoon," the lady answers.

"But that's impossible. I had an appointment with him and a client this morning," Jeri glances at her wrist, "in about seven minutes."

The lady makes a show of checking her computer and then the hand-written giant calendar on her desk. Her fingertip slows. "Aha. You must be Jeri," she says with a triumphant grin, but Jeri is having none of her friendliness.

"I have an appointment this morning. I drove an hour to get here," she says.

The lady looks confused. "Did you not get a phone call from your client?"

Jeri feels embarrassed, a feeling she hates. She glances at her cell phone before holding it up for the lady to see. "Do you see any missed calls in there for today because I don't," she barks.

The lady raises her hands in the air. "Hey, I'm just asking a question. I'm not Caden. Don't yell at me."

The familiarity in the woman's voice with the sound of

Caden's name on her lips pokes at Jeri, and, try as she might, she can't ignore it. "Do you know the client?" she asks, hoping she sounds professional, even though the lady stating his name just changed the dynamics of the entire conversation.

The clerk looks caught. "It's not my job to make calls on behalf of the client to the bail bonds agent," she answers stiffly.

"That's not what I asked," Jeri argues.

"Regina," a man's voice booms from somewhere behind Jeri who turns to meet it.

She takes in the robe he's tugging on over his button-up shirt and slacks. "Judge. I'm Jeri White," she says.

"Jeri. Come on into my chambers. Let's have a chat," he says as if they are old friends.

Jeri doesn't want to make nice with the Judge. They just met, and she's pretty sure she's being placated. That's the only thing she hates more than being talked to as if she's a weaker sex, which is what the Judge is doing right now. Jeri tells herself the only reason she's following this man is for the good of her client; that and the Judge is old enough to be her grandpa, which is the only reason she's letting him talk to her as if she were completely clueless and doesn't understand the definition of common courtesy. Which is something Caden knows nothing about. Which must be the reason he didn't call her this morning. These thoughts assail Jeri as she follows the Judge through his courtroom, down two steps, and then down two steps more. By the time he turns the tiny doorknob that looks out of place attached to an overly tall door, she's more than a little fired up.

The Judge steps behind his huge desk and sits down in

his chair. "Have a seat," he says as he waves his hand out in front of him.

Jeri crosses her arms on her chest. "No, thank you, Judge. I'd rather stand."

The Judge gives her a slow smile. "I take it you're unhappy that your client did not call you to let you know he can't make it to court this morning."

Understanding sinks in. "But he called you," Jeri says.

The Judge leans back in his chair. "Yes. He called me. I am the Judge, and it affected my schedule, so—"

Jeri is so mad she's fuming. "It affects my schedule too, you know."

The Judge taps his hands on the desk. "I'm sure it was an emergency. I don't believe Caden would have *not* called you on purpose," he says, but there's a bit of teasing in his voice, and Jeri is infuriated.

"And you know this because you know him so well?" she spits out.

By the look of incredulity on the Judge's face, it's safe to say he is not used to being spoken to in this manner. "I can see that you will not be happy until you see Caden for yourself, so let me give you the address where he can be found," he says as he scribbles something on an index card and passes it over to her. "You'd better wear a hard hat and some rubber boots, missy."

Jeri snatches the index card off his desk and shoves it in her cardigan sweater pocket. She's so angry she can't see straight. "Where would I find a pair of rubber boots?"

The Judge stares at her from behind his bifocals. His blue eyes sparkle and shine. "Head over to the hardware store. They ought to have some."

Jeri stands up and spins around. Her long skirt whooshes

and twirls. "I'm not kiddin' bout those rubber boots, lady. You wouldn't want to get those fancy Freebirds of yours in the dirt. It's muddy where you're goin', and there are some things you can't wash off leather."

Jeri pauses. The Judge sees more than his old eyes and slow ways of speaking and walking let on. "How'd you know these are Freebirds?"

He chuckles. "I buy my wife a pair every year. They're her weakness."

"It's really that messy, huh," Jeri says as she softens her tone.

"Where Caden's working? Yeah. Better tuck that long skirt of yours into those long rubber boots, or you'll be carrying all kinds of our small-town crap back with you to the city," he jokes.

Jeri raises an eyebrow. "You got something against the city, Judge?"

He shakes his full head of silver hair. "No, hon. Not really. I love visiting cities. I like the culture. I like the variety. But, at the end of the day, I prefer to live the quiet life. I like knowing my neighbors. When my kids were growing up it was nice to know if one of them got in a little trouble, most people were interested in redirecting them and trying to keep them out of it."

Jeri tosses a hand on her hip. "Small towns are also hotbeds for gossip. Everyone is in everybody's business. You're a judge. You oughta know that better than anyone."

He laughs out loud. "Perhaps, but I can tell you this. Anything that happens in my courtroom stays in my courtroom. These lips are sealed."

Her eyes narrow. She gives him a direct stare. "Including what's going on right now?" she questions.

His eyes light with excitement. Jeri is a little worried. "We're in my office, Jeri. Court is not in session."

Jeri's stomach tightens at the way this conversation turned on her. She feels like the Judge is going to give Caden a call as soon as she leaves his office. She hates the thought of someone getting one over on her. Her fists clench inside her sweater pockets. Caden may know the Judge, and he may have everyone in his small town in his pocket, but Caden Brown is going down.

Jeri walks to the Judge's tall door and grips the doorknob. "It would have been nice if someone would have called me and saved me the drive over here this morning. I have other work to get done too," she states in a not-so-nice fashion.

"I understand, and I'm sorry you wasted a trip driving over," the Judge pauses, "but something tells me this trip means a little more to you than the others." He holds her gaze. "You might discover living in a small town isn't all that bad."

Jeri's jaw drops. She wonders if Caden talked to the Judge about her. Surely not. "The only thing this small town means to me is some people in it can be a real pain in my ass," she growls. "And he's not going to have much of one when I get done with him," she vows before she rips the door open and lets it fall shut on its own. She's halfway across the courtroom in seconds, but she can't outrun the sound of the Judge's laughter as it trails her down the flight of the stairs and through the front door of the courthouse.

The Judge's eyes water. He's still laughing as he stands beside a courthouse window to watch the tiny woman in her long sweater, long skirt, and hair pulled back in a tight bun about as tight as the purse in her lips when she walked into his office.

"Oh boy. Caden's gonna get an earful this mornin'," he says with a smile on his face. "If I was twenty years younger, I'd tail her out to the worksite and pull up a lawn chair. I have a feelin' there's gonna be fireworks." He chuckles at his own words and gives a heavy sigh. "Young love. There's nothin' like it."

eight

Jeri whips her Spark car around the corner at lightning speed. She flies down Main Street just below the maximum speed limit, ignoring the looks from pedestrians on the sidewalk staring at her madness as she keeps her eyes peeled for the local hardware store.

"That Judge better not have been tellin' me a whopper," she growls. About the time she thinks she's been fooled again, she spies the orange awning sporting a big black hammer. "Arm Yourselves" is written below it in bold, black lettering. Jeri giggles in spite of her anger.

"That's pretty good," she says as she hops out of her car, hitting the lock button on her key fob out of habit before striding toward the front door with an outstretched hand, but a man beats her to it. He holds the door open, and she walks through.

"Thank you," she says as kind as she can manage before she steps inside and starts down the aisles of hoses.

"May I help you?" a friendly woman dressed in faded over-alls, a heather gray tee shirt, and adorable flowery hiking boots pops up at her right side while Jeri scans the left side of the aisle. Jeri can't help but smile. She thinks she may have met a fellow shoe lover as she meets the curious gaze of a pair of dark brown eyes that match the lady's dark curls waving this way and that as they frame her heart-shaped face.

"Yes, I'm looking for tall rubber boots."

"Doing some gardening?" the lady asks.

Jeri is just about to tell this lady it's none of her business, but she changes her mind. If Caden doesn't want his business all over town, maybe he shouldn't stand her up on their first appointment. "No, actually, I'm tracking down a guy who had a professional appointment with me today, and he didn't show. So I'm going out to the mines to find him."

The lady's lip trembles just a hair. "Oh, dear. I hope he's okay. We've all been praying for the miners this morning after that awful event." She pauses, and Jeri thinks she might be waiting for her to say more, but Jeri doesn't. "Thank goodness they all got out in time," she adds. She leans over and grabs a pair of boots that look more like hiking boots and holds them out. "Here. You'll want something more durable if you're going out there. The landscape is a bit rocky."

Jeri feels slightly intimidated by her words, but she's still annoyed that Caden hasn't called her yet. "Thanks," she says as she takes them from the woman and carries them up to the empty counter to pay.

A second or two later, the lady is back. "That'll be $37.99." Jeri sticks her credit card in the machine. The lady writes her a receipt. Jeri raises her eyebrows in question. "We still like to keep a touch of the past in our business dealings. So we write out paper receipts," the lady says with a smile.

She sticks her hand out with a smile on her face. "I'm Jane Landon, and this is my store."

Jeri points toward the front door. "I like your awning. Arm Yourselves. That's clever."

Jane giggles. "That was my idea. Sometimes home projects or life in general can feel quite daunting, so I thought why not have a little fun and practicality in my store name?"

Jeri holds up her boots. "I'm trying to be prepared." She remembers the Judge's other suggestion. "You don't happen to have a hard hat, do you?"

Jane grins. "As a matter of fact, I do." She ducks down behind the counter and comes up with one. She holds it out. "Here."

Jeri reaches for her purse again. "How much do I owe you?"

Jane's grin slips a little. "You can't buy this one. It's not for sale, but you can borrow it."

Jeri is confused. "We just met. How do you know I'll bring it back?"

Jane waves her hand. "If you don't have time to return it, give it to whatever miner you're razzing this morning," she says with an ornery grin.

Jeri's face flushes a little. "Is it that obvious?"

Jane giggles. "I recognize a woman on a mission when I see one," she says with a wink. "You don't have to tell me what it's about. I figure it must be pretty darn important if you're going to all this trouble."

Jeri grabs the hat. "Thanks," she says as she walks out the door before she changes her mind. She can't believe how much trouble she's going to for one client, but she refuses to examine that thought any further. "I always get my man," she reasons as she climbs into her car. She plugs the address the Judge gave her into her GPS system. "Let's go, Sparky," she says to her dash. "Onto our next adventure."

Fifteen minutes later, Jeri questions the wisdom of her decision as she drives down the dirt road, dodging rocks that are about a fourth the size of the wheels on her tiny car, but she keeps going. She pulls into the far end of the small lot of parked cars. She scans the area but doesn't see Caden's bike. "I'm here. I may as well get out," she grumps. She opens the door, wraps her prairie skirt around her knees and exchanges her Freebirds for her newly-purchased hiking boots. She stands up, leans over, and concentrates on shoving her long skirt into her hiking boots, but it's not working. The slippery material of her skirt keeps sneaking out of her boots. She jams the hard hat on her head, her cell phone in her pocket, her keys in her other pocket, and slams her car door. She gathers a fistful of skirt in each hand and heads for the group of men in the distance.

She feels more foolish the closer she gets. She knows she ought to turn around and go home, but she can't. She has to see Caden. She slows her walk the last six feet or so. The men turn in her direction. Her eyes rove over the group of miners that grows larger the closer she gets, but she already knows. Caden isn't among them. Anxiety pings off her insides, and she doesn't understand it because it has nothing to do with the fact that he missed their appointment.

If Jeri were more aware of their stares, she might notice the looks of appreciation from more than a few miners, as she stands before them in her hard hat tilted slightly to the side as it sits atop her signature bun. A soft breeze passes by, shaking a few stray hairs loose from her bun, and her blonde hair sticks to the side of her cheek. Her hazel eyes widen in irritation as the wind tosses her skirt around, and air hits the back of her knees.

She opens her mouth to inquire about Caden but closes it as she sees a form in the distance walking out of what looks like a black hole. She heads straight for him, absent-mindedly creating a path through the middle of the men. His head is ducked. His broad shoulders are hunched, as if they carry the weight of the mess behind him. She can't walk fast enough to get to him.

"Caden," she says.

His head pops up. Water runs down his face. He looks confused. "Jeri?" he says her name, and it sounds out of place. "What are you doing here?" A small smile pops out. "Did you come out to see if I'm okay?"

Even though that's exactly what she feels, she's annoyed at his words, but more than that, she's rendered temporarily speechless by his soaking wet form and his removing of his jacket, and then another lighter jacket, followed by a heavy sweatshirt. He's down to a thin, white v-neck tee shirt that's plastered to his very fit form.

"I came out here because you didn't show up in court this morning," she says loud enough for the guys behind her to hear, a fact she knows, because she hears more than a few laughs. This incenses her further, along with the fact that her brain doesn't want to work because it's stuck on how Caden looks in his wet shirt.

"I had an emergency. It couldn't be avoided," he grounds out from between his chattering teeth. Just as she suspected, he doesn't enjoy being scolded in front of his crew, a fact she should have known if her mouth and anger didn't run away with her at the very sight of this infuriating man who makes her want to kiss him out of gratefulness that he's okay. These feelings shake her to the core. His withering look tells her he's about to brush her off, and she's mad all over again. "I'm sorry that I missed our *date*," he emphasizes, as if to be sure she understands her job is of minuscule importance compared to his, "but there were lives at stake this morning," he says as he waves in the general direction of the group of men with a shaking hand. His lips look as if they're turning blue.

"You could have called," she says in a quieter voice.

"You're mad at me because I didn't call you," he all but roars, and Jeri catches movement in the corner of her eye. Her embarrassment burns clean through when she sees the group of men slowly turn their back on her.

Her eyes water. She can't believe this idiotic man is about to make her cry. Jeri has never cried over a guy, not even when Miles cheated on her. She's not about to now. She pokes him in his hard, unforgiving chest, and she wishes she did not know what it felt like about the time she does it. He reaches for her hand, but she slaps his away as she points a finger in the direction of his face. Her eyes meet his.

"Had you called me, you would have saved me the headache of a trip and driving out to your podunk town which is as much as a pain in my butt as these stupid rocks I'm standing on in your stupid parking lot," she growls. He says nothing as he starts walking toward the guys. "Where are you going?" she demands as she trails after him.

"I'm going to get d-dry clothes," he stutters.

Jeri walk-jogs to keep up with his long strides. "I have a workday too, you know," she chides. "I may not be dragging people out of holes in the ground or swimming in whatever you were this morning but that doesn't mean what I do isn't important," she argues as they walk along. "If it weren't for me, you'd still be sitting in a jail cell right now," she reminds him.

He stops in his steps to give her a fiery glare. "Trust me, sweetheart, I'd kind of like to be in a jail cell right now."

His term of endearment ticks her off. She grabs a hold of his upper arm. A bolt of awareness shoots through both of them as strong as an electric shock. She lets go. "I'm nobody's sweetheart," she states.

He stops beside an old Honda Civic, opens the door, and whips off his shirt before toweling himself off. "You got that right." He starts to unbutton his pants, and she whips around to face the other direction.

"Are you just going to strip here in the parking lot?" she squeaks.

"Normally there's no one here but us guys, and I'm not walking around in wet briefs all day, so yeah. I guess I am," he says without an ounce of apology.

"Tell me when you're decent," she grumps.

"I'm decent all day long, Jeri. I can't say the same for you," he grumbles.

His words steal her breath for half a second. She's never been so insulted. "I'm just trying to do my job."

"You could have called me. You didn't need to come all the way out here just to chew my ass in front of my crew," he growls.

"You could have sent me a text to tell me you weren't going to make it to court," she argues.

"I let the Judge know," he offers.

She wheels around, she's so mad. She's relieved to see he's partially clothed, but he's still shirtless as he stands in front of her towel-drying his hair. Jeri suspects by the light in his eyes he has some idea how much she appreciates the view and how the sight of his bare chest flusters her.

"That's not how the chain of command works," she supplies. "You're supposed to call me, and then I call the courthouse," she says as her voice trails off, because she's caught like a fish in a net between the twinkle in his eye, the curve of his perfect lips, and the dip in his collarbone. He rests his arm on his open Honda door while he stands before her in his faded blue jeans and untied boots, looking very much like a calendar boy, right down to the knowing smile on his slightly stubbled chin covered by a five o'clock shadow. Jeri is torn between running back to Sparky in retreat or snapping fifty pictures in freeze-frame.

"Thanks for that helpful reminder, *boss*," he says in an overly suggestive tone that tells her he's well aware of who's in control of their uneven relationship.

Jeri forces herself to reorient. "You're welcome. I've got to go."

She spins around to leave, clutching at her skirt the way she's been doing since she got there, but she remembers her hard hat. She spins around once more and removes the hat. "Here. This belongs to Jane at the hardware store. Do you mind returning it to her?"

Caden tugs the bottom part of his tee shirt down. He takes a hold of the hat. "You could ask nicely," he says with a straight face.

Jeri resists the urge to roll her eyes. "Please."

Caden tosses it in his car and reaches in for another shirt. He shrugs into a heavy flannel. His eyes look past her. "You've got a flat tire," he states.

Jeri turns and looks. "Dang it," she mutters. She knows

how to change a tire, but it'll take her forever. She heads for her car. Caden walks beside her. "What are you doing?"

"Changing your tire," he says in a tone that tells her he's not the least bit happy about it.

"I can do it myself," she argues.

"I'm sure you can, but since you drove all the way out here just for me even though I didn't ask you to, I guess it's partially my fault," he states as if it's a normal thing for women to drive an hour-and-a-half out of their way to see him on a regular basis. Jeri would be more offended at his words if she didn't believe they were true.

"Thank you," she manages as she hits the button on her key fob to unlock her car. She holds the button down for the trunk that slowly opens.

Caden raises an eyebrow at the amount of stuff piled to the ceiling in the back of her tiny car as he starts to unload it. Jeri races after him. "Please stop. I'll stack it how I want it," she adds as she hurries to rearrange the pile he's already made on the ground. "There are certain things I don't want to touch the ground," she explains from her squat beside him.

"I don't have a lot of time. I need to get back to the guys," he explains.

"I didn't ask you to change my tire," she argues as he drops the tire on the ground and reaches for her tire iron.

Jeri stands off to the side as he jacks up her tiny car. "So have you always lived in this town?" she asks, although she's pretty sure she knows the answer.

"Yep."

"Was your dad a miner?"

"Yep."

"And your grandpa?" she continues.

"Yep." He turns to look at her. "Is there a point to all this questioning?"

Jeri leans back on her heels. "Not really. I'm just curious."

He looks her up and down. "Was your mom a bail bondswoman?"

Jeri giggles. "Definitely not. My mother was a stay-at-home mom."

He nods his head. "And her mother?"

"Stay-at-home mom," Jeri answers. "Pretty standard stuff."

"So I'm guessing they're not exactly thrilled with your choice of profession," he drawls.

"Not particularly, no," she answers, "but I figure if my career choice is my one rebellion, it's not the worst thing."

Caden chuckles at her words. "That's not the line of logic I would necessarily follow, but I suppose I see your point."

Jeri sighs. "It's not like I grew up thinking I wanted to be a bail bondswoman," she states.

"Then how did you get into it?" Caden asks.

Jeri fidgets. "I was at a crossroads. I had three years of college behind me, but I still had no idea what I wanted to do with my life." She takes a deep breath. "There was a girl who lived in the apartment next to me. She seemed to have that part of her life figured out, so I asked her what she did for a living. She told me. I told her she was crazy. She challenged me. She told me to come spend a week with her at her job to see if it was something I thought I would like to do. I didn't have anything better to do, so I did. It wasn't so much the job that appealed to me, but her. She believed in me. She told me she was looking for a partner, and she thought I'd make a good one, and so we started working together."

Caden nods his head. "So it was more about your friendship."

Jeri nods. "Yes."

"And is she still working with you?" Caden asks.

Jeri smiles down at him. "She is. You met her. It's Charmaine. She's a real character. She can come off kind of strong, but she's got a good heart."

Caden tightens the lug nuts one more time. "Well. I'm glad you have a co-worker you can trust. That makes a big difference." He says between grunts at his efforts before he stands up, tosses the flat tire in the back, and lays the tire iron back in place. He turns to look down at Jeri. She looks up at him.

The silence grows more awkward the longer it goes on. He takes a few steps closer until the edges of her skirt brush against his denim-covered shins. His booted toes bump against hers. "If you wanted to see me, all you had to do was call," he says in a quiet voice that grazes her earlobes and muddles her brain before it travels down every nerve ending, heating her clean through.

"I didn't want to see you," she says in a breathy tone. "I had to."

A slow smile spreads across his face. "Exactly," he says as he traces the nape of her neck with his calloused finger before turning and walking away with his signature swagger.

Jeri frowns. "That's not what I meant," she answers to his back.

"*That's what I heard*," he calls out in response.

She busies herself shoving everything back in her trunk. "This was so stupid. He's so dumb. Next time he can just deal with the Judge himself," she grumps, before she feels stupid all over again. "Duh. He did deal with the Judge himself. That's what got me into this mess in the first place," she gripes as she turns the key in the ignition. "Caden Brown is a royal pain in my butt," she continues. "I just wish he didn't look so good doing it," she says as she stares at the back of him one last time before she slowly turns her car around and hopes she doesn't get another flat tire on the way back to civilization.

Her phone buzzes. She checks it and realizes she's missed about four calls from Charmaine. "Oh, crap," she says as she answers. "Hey, Charmaine."

"Girl. Are you okay? I see you're out in the middle of nowhere."

"What? How?"

"SnapChat. It tells me where you are," Charmaine says.

"That's not creepy," Jeri mutters. "I'm sorry about that. I had an appointment with Caden. He stood me up," she grumps.

"Oh, boy. Did you tattoo his fine b'hind?" Charmaine asks with way too much enthusiasm.

"Let's just say I wasn't happy with him, and he knows it," Jeri replies.

Charmaine giggles in the phone. "This is a story. I can tell."

Jeri smiles in spite of everything she's gone through in one morning. "Are you ready to hear it?"

There's silence on the other end. "Charmaine?" Jeri asks, but she gets nothing. She sighs and keeps on driving but doesn't end the call. Charmaine will let her know when she's back. Jeri thinks things through, and the longer she does, the more she knows she might be in trouble. She's never lost her head the way she does whenever she's around Caden.

"I'm back," Charmaine says in a breathless tone. "I had to go get some snacks and a drink."

"For what?" Jeri questions.

"For the rest of the story," Charmaine replies, as if it's perfectly normal to make a vending machine run before finishing a phone call.

"Okay. Well, first of all, Caden called the Judge, and neither of them called me," Jeri states.

"Oh, no he didn't," Charmaine says in her usual attitude-girl fashion.

"Oh, yes he di-id," Jeri says right back.

"Ooh, girl. This is gonna be good," Charmaine adds. "Proceed."

Jeri takes a deep breath as she gets back on the main highway. "As I was say-ing, first he called the Judge, and then he didn't show up at the courthouse," she goes on. Jeri relays her morning to the best of her entertaining ability to Charmaine for the next twenty minutes. Charmaine shows her appreciation by remaining uncharacteristically quiet, for the most part.

"He was dripping wet? That's sex-y," she interjects.

"That's not the point I was making," Jeri said, but she doesn't dispute Charmaine's opinion.

"He changed your tire? That's so romantic," Charmaine swoons.

"I didn't ask him to," Jeri says, but her heart isn't in the argument.

"He sounds like a real gentleman," Charmaine says, and she almost sounds wistful.

"Yeah," Jeri mostly agrees. "Except that he didn't call me to tell me he wasn't going to make our appointment."

"It was an emergency. For all you know, he had to swim

out of that mine," Charmaine says. "He's kind of like a hero," she adds in an awe-filled tone.

"I wouldn't go that far," Jeri argues.

"He's definitely not like the criminals we bail out every day," Charmaine keeps up.

"Okay, okay. No, he's not," Jeri reluctantly agrees.

"So what're you gonna do about him?" Charmaine asks.

"What do you mean?" Jeri replies as her anxiety starts to rise again. She has no idea. The only thing she knows is she wants to keep seeing him.

"Are you just going to let him go?" Charmaine keeps up.

Jeri blushes from head to toe. "Are you asking me if I'm going to ask the guy out on a date?" she demands.

Charmaine's quiet for a second or two. "Yeah. That's what I'm sayin'," she encourages.

"Um, no. First of all, he's my client, and second of all, I don't ask guys out. They ask me," Jeri says.

"But you've dated a couple of jerks," Charmaine protests. "This guy seems nice. He's like the real deal."

"It's a good thing we're such good friends, or I might take offense," Jeri mumbles. "And nice guys don't like girls to ask them out. They think it's too forward."

"Then maybe just let him know you're interested," Charmaine suggests.

"And how do I do that?" Jeri barks because she doesn't like the way this conversation is going, and she feels like her best friend has turned on her.

"You could start with bein' nice. You don't have to argue all the time, you know," Charmaine says in an accusatory tone.

"I wouldn't argue with him if he wasn't so difficult to work with," Jeri spits out.

"That's it. That's all I've got. I gotta go. I got another call," Charmaine says before the call ends.

Jeri ends the call through her steering wheel. "I'm not the one who's being difficult. It's him. All he had to do was call me," she grumps as she pulls into the parking lot behind her office. She picks up her phone and scrolls through the multiple missed calls from other clients. "Crap. I can't lose all my other clients because of one stubborn jackass," she grumbles as she sticks her feet out and unlaces the hiking boots before pulling her feet out of them. She opens the back door and sets them inside before sliding into her Freebirds once more. She reaches in her messenger bag for her signature notebook and starts writing down all her missed calls by name, phone number, date, and time. Sometimes it's easier to focus when she's not in the same room as her noisy co-worker who she loves dearly but can't think over, especially when Charmaine's in a mood.

Jeri feels a little less anxious when she gets to the end of her twenty-four missed calls written down in front of her in chronological order with three spaces in between each one to allow for note-taking following each conversation. She drops her notebook back in her messenger bag, locks her door, and walks inside.

She reaches the top of the stairs and opens the door to the main office. Charmaine sits at her desk with her back to her friend. "I'm just going to use the conference room. I've got phone calls to make," Jeri says to her friend's back. Charmaine does nothing to acknowledge her presence, but this is standard procedure when Charmaine has her back up about something, so Jeri doesn't think anything of it as she heads for the small room no bigger than a closet, but it has a phone and a closed door that provides a little bit of silence and privacy.

A few hours and twenty-four phone calls later, Jeri feels a little lighter and a little heavier at the same time. Her phone calls are all done, but she's got a full day tomorrow, starting with thirteen meetings in front of the judge at the city courthouse; but at least her clients will show up for her this time, she thinks to herself. "Thank goodness for lawbreakers. That's thirteen thousand dollars I didn't have yesterday," she mutters.

There's a knocking at her door. Who could that be? Charmaine doesn't knock. Jeri opens the door to the windowless closet space. A bouquet of flowers greets her. A dark-haired messenger boy peeks around the side. "Are you Jeri White?"

"Yes," Jeri says, and she can't help but smile. It's been so long since she received flowers.

"Then these are for you," he says with a grin. She takes the vase in both hands and walks toward her desk.

There's a throat clearing behind her. "This is also for you," he says.

She hurriedly sets the flowers down and returns to his side. He holds out a baggie full of what looks like dirt. "What's that?"

He shrugs his shoulders. "I don't know. He just said to give it to you."

Jeri frowns. "Thank you."

The boy grins at her. "You're welcome. Have a nice day," he adds before spinning around and hurrying for the door.

"You could've tipped him," Charmaine says. "He was kind of cute."

Jeri wrinkles her nose. "He looked like he was still in high school, Charmaine. That's kind of young. Even for you," she scolds.

Charmaine rolls her eyes. "The good thing about young guys is you can still train 'em to treat you right." She eyes Jeri's flowers. "You gonna read that card or?"

Jeri feels bad because she thinks she hears a little jealousy in Charmaine's tone. "Yeah, sorry," she says as she holds up the thin baggie of dirt. She squeezes the outside of it, trying to feel if there's something hidden in the middle of all the dirt. She can't tell.

"I'm sorry I didn't call. Here's some dirt for you to fling at me the next time we meet. At least I'll know what's coming —Caden" Jeri reads his message more than once. Each time she reads it she's torn between laughing out loud at his clever joke and being mad because he's making light of her anger over him standing her up.

"Well? What does it say?" Charmaine demands.

She tosses the card at Charmaine and plops down at her desk. "The guy is so annoying."

Charmaine giggles over the card. "You gonna text him to say thank you?"

Jeri stares up at the beautiful arrangement of Gerbera daisies, baby's breath, and other greenery encased in a dark blue vase with a bright yellow M stamped right in the middle. She can't help but smile a little despite his ornery remark.

"Wolverines," she whispers, but her mind travels to Caden's brown hair darkened by the water and his shaking musculature form defined by his water-soaked clothing. As much as she hates to admit it, there was a hint of Hugh Jackman's dark character, a conflicted hero who is no man to mess with. Jeri shakes her head to erase those crazy thoughts. She's clearly losing her mind if she's comparing Caden to Wolverine.

"I don't know," she answers. "I can't decide if the card was a compliment or an insult."

Charmaine giggles. "Sounds like he's got you tied in knots," she teases.

Jeri grabs up her stuff. "I'm going to the gym," she announces.

Charmaine glances at the clock. "It's four-forty-five. You never leave before five o'clock," she reprimands.

Jeri rolls her eyes. "Like you don't skip out of here plenty of days at three-forty-five" she pops off.

"That's cause I gotta grab a table for my girls and get our appetizers ordered before four PM so they're half price," she reasons.

Jeri shrugs as she stops at the office door and turns to face Charmaine. "Makes no difference to me when you leave. I'm just sayin.'"

She raises an eyebrow at her friend as she takes in yet another outlandish outfit. Charmaine sits in her corduroy jean skirt held together by five fat buttons that go right up the middle. Her maroon blouse slides around on her rounded caramel-colored shoulders. Her legs that are not in the most lady-like position, especially considering her skirt slowly inches up her thighs, are encased in knit tights decorated with vibrant poppies and stems. "Love your outfit," Jeri says and bites her tongue so she doesn't tell her friend her skirt's climbing. That would make her feel like a scolding grandma.

Charmaine tilts her head to the side, causing all of her curls spilling out the top of her high ponytail to swing off to one side. "Thanks." Her big brown eyes rove up and down Jeri, taking in yet another prairie skirt, solid-colored knit blouse, and long sweater. "I like..." she pauses long enough to be a little snarky, "your Freebirds," she adds.

Jeri holds in a giggle at her friend's unspoken boredom at her ability to wear the same clothes everyday week in and week out, but she doesn't care. They're comfortable. They're reliable. They're dependable. Jeri likes all of those things.

"You ever think about wearing bigger hoops?" Charmaine encourages. "You know, like Julia Stiles in *Save the Last Dance*?"

Jeri stares her down. "I'm not some secret hip-hop dance girl trying to catch a brotha." Charmaine raises an eyebrow in warning. Jeri's gaze doesn't waver. "I'm just using your language like you use mine," she argues. "And I don't have anything against brothas," she says even as the word feels weird on her lips. "They're just not my type."

Charmaine sniffs. "I don't know if I should feel offended."

Jeri laughs out loud. "Trust me, girl. You should not. I'm too boring for a brotha."

Charmaine frowns again. "I don't know about that. You had a guy practically climbin' out of the water to get to you this mornin', and then he's doin' a strip tease in the parkin' lot which you totally should've watched by the way."

Jeri wrinkles her nose. "Um, no thank you."

Charmaine continues as if Jeri didn't answer. "And the guy rides a motorcycle. How hot is that?"

Jeri grows more uncomfortable at the exaggerated picture Charmaine draws of Caden, which is the whole reason she needs to get to the gym and be gone before he shows up. "See you tomorrow. I gotta go," she says as she points to the clock. "It's five o'clock now, boss," she teases.

nine

Caden pounds out another lap at the outside track that encircles the gym. It was a strange set-up at the beginning, and it still looks funny when you pull into the small parking lot through the driveway that is a brief break in the track just wide enough for cars to drive in and out of, but it feels good to be able to run outside. He's clear across the way when he sees the pale, yellow car pull in.

"That's just terrific," he mutters as he keeps up his pace.

He runs as if he's trying to escape something or someone, but it's not working. Every time he rounds the far end of the track, all he can see is her tiny immovable car staring back at him just like she does. "This is stupid. I'm just going to do some lunges and jumping jacks and call it a day," he says to the empty track as he tries to catch his breath while he does a wind-down walking lap. "No. I'm not staying out of the gym just because she's in there. I can go in and lift weights if I want to. She doesn't own the gym," he reasons. He rubs his upper arms as he ponders. "But my arms did get a workout this morning from the lifting and the bit of swimming," he reasons. "I've had a long day already." He's almost talked himself out of going back in. "But she didn't even say thank you for the flowers," he argues. "That's kind of rude." He says as he walks across the field toward the back door of the gym.

He waves the magnetic device set in his rubber wristband in front of the door. When they first came out with the wristbands, he thought the idea was sort of lame, but when he realized he didn't have to carry his keys around the track when he jogged, he bought a couple of wristbands to keep in his gym bag. He spots her blonde bun atop her head bobbing up and down as she goes to town on the elliptical. He senses the tension in her from across the room, and he'd like to think he put it there. Kind of. He kind of feels bad about it, but not bad enough as he starts toward her but stops. He walks over to his side of the gym, the weights. He changes his routine just a bit as he puts less weight than usual on the bar to do his reps. He lays down on the inclined bench and lifts.

Caden keeps a sneaky eye on Jeri periodically to be sure he doesn't miss her leaving. He thinks he's doing a pretty good job until he looks around the gym and realizes she's not there. He all but tosses the medicine ball with all the others and gets up off the floor. He rushes over to her car, but she's not in it. He's all alone in an empty lot. He feels clueless, and he doesn't like the feeling. Now that he's out here, he's not going back in until he sees her. He's committed. He leans on the back end of her Spark car. A high-pitched beeping starts. Caden can't believe he set off the alarm.

As fast as it started it stops. Caden looks in the direction of the gym but sees no one. He starts to scan the area. He spots Jeri jogging across the occasionally busy street with her key fob in hand. She looks a bit upset.

"Geez. What did I do this time?" Caden mumbles.

"Why did you set off my car alarm?" Jeri demands as she jogs up to her car.

Caden crosses his arms on his chest. "I didn't mean to," he offers. "I was waiting for you," he says.

"Why?" she demands.

"Did you get anything interesting today?"

Jeri's face lights up briefly before she shuts down right in front of him. "Yeah. I got a baggie full of dirt."

Caden smirks. "Did you now?"

Jeri frowns at his teasing. "Yeah, I did."

"And did you open it?" he asks.

"No," she says in a confused tone of voice.

"Ah. If you had you would know it smells like coffee," he says.

"Because?" she says. She has no idea where this conversation is going.

"Because if I'm going to have dirt thrown at me it may as well smell good," he says. "And if you should decide not to throw it at me, everyone knows coffee grounds help flowers grow,' he adds.

"They do not," she says. "They're strictly there for pleasing the senses."

Caden's whole demeanor changes. He turns Hugh Jackman dark as he steps closer to her. He lays a hand on top of her Spark car as he leans close to her ear. "And do I, Jeri? Do I please your senses?" he all but whispers.

Jeri inhales at the same time her mind tells her not to, because she knows what she will discover—Caden's manly scent that is as evident as the sweat circle attached to his tee shirt collar that grows as they speak. She gives him a shove.

"I'm not going to answer that," she says. "It's a ridiculous question," she continues from her driver's seat that she seeks refuge inside the car. Her door is half-shut. "Thank you for the flowers. They were lovely," she says in the most stiff, detached voice as possible. "And thank you for the coffee dirt," she adds as she tries to pull her door shut, but Caden's lower arm and hand prevent her from doing so.

Caden drills her with his stare. "So what happens now?"

Jeri blinks a few times. "I don't know. Why don't you ask the Judge," she pops off.

Caden tosses his head back and laughs. "That would be breaking the chain of command," he teases.

Jeri eyes his hand, the thickness of his forearm, and the tightness in his bicep as he holds her car door open despite the fact she's trying to shut it. He's clearly an obstruction, but it doesn't feel threatening, which is strange. Jeri suspects Caden knows he's a presence she cannot ignore.

"I'm sure your hands are quite capable of breaking many things," she argues before closing her mouth because she didn't mean to say those thoughts aloud. She stares straight ahead, refusing to meet his amused gaze. "Mr. Brown, if you would kindly let go of my door, I'd like to go home," she says in a stiff tone that suggests spinster-schoolmarm as well as her back that is straight as a board.

Caden stares a second too long. "As you wish," he says before closing the door quietly while the small inner door between him and Jeri residing inside his mind that he thought was opening slams in his face at her overly polite tone. He knows she's not afraid of him, at least not in a bad way. He thinks she's afraid of her feelings because he doesn't know what else keeps her from being friendlier when there's an obvious attraction between the two of them.

But it's more than an attraction. Caden is certain. There's

a connection. And he's not letting her go so easily, which has to be the only reason he finds himself driving over to her uncle's place. Caden is frustrated to find her car parked outside. He doesn't want her to think he's following her, because this was merely accidental, or was it?

Maybe there is such a thing as fate, and maybe the universe is pushing them together, he thinks but doesn't say. No one talks like that anymore. Although Caden's mother is a definite believer in such romanticism, somehow, he doesn't think Jeri will be as receptive.

Caden fights the urge to stop by her uncle's apartment or her house. He heads for the bar that he hasn't set foot in since the night he was arrested, which was less than two weeks ago. But it feels like longer, especially considering how attached he's already feeling to Jeri. He recalls Saul's teasing him about when you know you know, but now he's not so sure Saul was joking. Caden's irritation with Jeri grows every time he thinks of the relief he saw in her face when he walked up on her all dripping wet. She was scared for him. He knows she was, so why is she so bent on hiding her feelings?

These thoughts swirl about in his head as he pulls up to the bar on his motorcycle and walks in. The first person he sees is baby-faced Bairn. Judging by his wide-eyed look of surprise followed by an immediate look of innocence that falls like a curtain, Bairn realizes Caden sees him. Caden's first reaction is rage, but then Jeri pops into his head. He wouldn't have met Jeri if he hadn't gotten thrown in jail, and he can't be sorry about that. Caden can't believe how fast his thoughts went straight to Jeri and how fast his bad mood lifted as a result.

He steps up to the bar and gives Owen a smile. "Hey,

Owen. I'll take a Bud Light." Owen eyes Caden for half a second before glancing off in Bairn's direction. "I'm not gonna have any trouble from you tonight, right?" he mostly teases.

"Nah, man. I have no desire to go back to jail," Caden says. "I got bailed out once, I don't think I have enough rich friends to get bailed out twice," he jokes.

Owen nods his head as he sets the glass of foamy beer down on the bar. "I hear that," right before he coughs into his hand "Incoming," is what Caden thinks he hears right before two or three guys bump into the back of him.

"Hey man, I'm so sorry," Bairn belts out in a loud, nasally tone of voice with a hard edge that says he's anything but sorry.

Caden sets one foot on the floor and turns super slow-mo on his bar stool. He looks down to meet Bairn's eye while he stands there like an idiot with his hands in the air and a tell-tale smirk on his face. "No harm, no foul, Bairn," Caden replies.

A look of disappointment crosses Bairn's face. He clearly didn't get the reaction he was hoping for. "Wanna take another shot at me, Caden? I'd be happy to toss your sorry ass in jail again," he taunts.

His words and tone grate on Caden's ears, but he's not dumb enough to fall for Bairn's empty threats. On the other hand, there's no laws against arguing. "You can't take a punch, Bairn. That's what got me tossed in jail," Caden says before taking a long drink of his beer.

As usual, Bairn is determined to dish out what he can't take. He shakes his head "That's not what happened. You cold-cocked me, and I wasn't ready," he whines.

Caden stands up to his full height. He stares Bairn down.

"You shoulda been ready since you punched me in the back as I was walking away. It was a gut reaction. You hit me. I hit you. That should have been the end of it, but you can't take things like a man, baby-faced Bairn," Caden says.

Bairn's pale face goes beet red. It's not like people don't know that's his nickname, but no one's actually ever called him that to his face. Caden can't believe he just did, but Bairn never knows when to shut up. Caden turns back to Owen and winks before he faces Bairn once more. "These bars have cameras you know. They catch everything. Anyone want to roll tape on the fight?" he asks in a voice louder than necessary.

Bairn stands in the middle of his four buddies who slowly retreat from his circle. "Nah, man. You're not worth the trouble," Bairn says to save face.

Caden takes a sudden step toward him, and Bairn jumps. Caden backs up and sits down on his bar stool once more. He takes a sip of his beer, but his eyes never leave Bairn's, who slowly disappears into the crowd. He turns back around on his barstool to face Owen. "Sorry about that, man, but he was getting on my nerves. I can't believe he has the nerve to show back up here after he tattled on me because I won the fight."

Owen raises his eyebrows. "Takes all kinds, man. It takes all kinds."

Caden laughs a little. "It sure does," he says as he finishes his beer.

"Want another?" Owen asks as he takes his empty glass.

"Nope. I'll take some water when you get a minute," Caden requests.

Owen's blue eyes light up. "You met someone."

Caden feels so transparent. "Why do you say that?"

"You haven't been in in a while, and you must be in a better mood because you're drinking less, and you didn't take Bairn's bait."

Caden knocks on the bar and lays down a twenty as Owen slides a glass of ice water with a lemon in it in his direction. "That's what makes you a good bartender. You know how to read people."

Owen shoves the twenty in his pocket. "Thanks for the tip. That beer was $8."

Caden sips the glass of water while he keeps an eye on the game. "I know what beer costs. I guess I'm feeling generous," he teases.

Owen gives him a knowing wink. "Like I said. You definitely met someone."

Caden drains the glass of water and stands up. "I know I met someone, but I'm not sure she does," he says as he heads for the bathroom. Minutes later, he walks by the bar on his way out. "See ya later," he says to Owen, as he raises his hand.

"She'll know soon enough," Owen yells at Caden's back as he heads for the front door. "*I know you*," he calls again as Caden's hand hits the outside door to the bar, and Caden smiles.

The ride home is dark and quiet, just like Caden likes. He jogs up the steps leading to his apartment and unlocks the door before crashing on the couch and turning on his favorite sports channel. But mainly he stares at the screen. For the first time in a long time, he feels lonely, and he knows the reason. Jeri White.

Caden feels like a creeper when he googles her name. He can't believe how many people have it, and how many of them are men. Halfway down the screen, her face pops up.

"Blame the Champagne," he reads aloud before he laughs a little at the company name. "That's pretty funny," he says as he stares at her happy face that smiles right back at him. "She's a little too shiny and happy to be a bail bondswoman," he muses before he googles their company name. Her face pops up next to a smiling African-American woman who is just as happy and youthful as Jeri. Toasting glasses of champagne and a bunch of confetti sit between their pictures. "Too big of a night out?" is written beneath the glasses. A diamond ring icon is a little farther down the page. "Give us a ring!" is written under that. Green dollar signs come next. "Call 1-800-bae-u-out!" is written beneath that.

"That's the happiest, girliest, bail bond website page I ever saw," Caden says. "It looks more like an advertisement for an engagement party or something to do with weddings," he continues. "Who knew gettin' thrown in jail could be so positive?" he jokes, about the time he remembers how he met Jeri and drops his phone on the couch. "Alright, maybe sometimes it's a good thing."

ten

Jeri's week flies by. She's had so many calls and bailouts she'd swear it was a full moon or St. Patty's Day, but it's the second week in May. There's nothing significant about her calendar except for every day Caden hasn't called, and that's too many consecutive days in a row. She knows he's her client, and she specifically told him that, more than once. She shouldn't be disappointed he listened to her warnings. She considers Charmaine's advice, but she can't. There's no way Jeri is calling Caden and asking him out on a date. Instead, she stares at her calendar and wishes he would call her, right after she wishes she didn't care so much that it's another Friday, and she has no plans for the weekend besides curling up on the couch with her dogs and reading a book.

"Whatever happened with Wolverine?" Charmaine teases, startling Jeri out of her reverie.

"I'm sorry, what?"

"You know, with the Judge and everything," she goes on.

"Oh, yeah. I guess they worked it out because I haven't heard anything from either of them."

Charmaine gives her a look. "You gonna call Julie, the P.O., and ask her about him?"

Jeri blushes at the thought. "You *seriously* want me to call his probation officer? Why don't I just wave a big flag that says *I'm desperate for a date* on it?"

Charmaine pffts at Jeri. "Girl, get over yourself. Number one, the guy is ho-ot. That does not make you desperate. That just makes you not seeing-impaired."

Jeri rolls her eyes. "What's number two?"

Charmaine looks confused. "Say what?"

"You said number one. What is number two?"

"Girl. You are stallin'. Stop it. Just give Julie a call. The woman is so busy, she'll just be happy you're offering her some help."

Jeri considers the suggestion. "Why would I do that? I've never done that," she adds in a panicky voice. "She would totally see right through me. It'd be so embarrassing."

"Okay, okay. Don't get your panties in a wad. I'll call her," Charmaine says before Jeri can respond.

Jeri is out of her chair. She leans over Charmaine who blocks the desk phone as if she's boxing out in a game of basketball.

"Hey, Julie," Charmaine crows. Jeri rolls her eyes. "How's it going, gi-rl. I know, I know. It's been a hot minute. Say, we..."

Jeri clears her throat and makes a fatal gesture with her finger and her neck at Charmaine, who promptly turns her back on Jeri. "*I* was wondering...did you happen to have any paperwork on a guy named Caden Brown?" She spins back around on her swivel chair to make wide eyes at Jeri, who glares at her in return. "You did? You don't have time to run over there? Well, there's two of us up here. We could deliver the message to him for you." She waves her hand in the air. "Sure, sure. No, it wouldn't be any trouble. No trouble at all. You know how it be up in here. All quiet and creepy. We live for excuses to leave the office." She tilts her head to the side and puckers her pink lips at Jeri before batting her blue magnetic eyelashes. "Sounds good. I'll keep an eye out for the fax. Girl, it ain't no thang. You have a good day. Nice talkin' to ya."

Charmaine hangs up her desk phone and levels Jeri with a withering stare. "You owe me. You're welcome."

Jeri opens her mouth to protest, but Charmaine points a long, jeweled lavender-colored nail at her. "And don't be actin' like I haven't seen you mopin' around half the mornin' like a lovesick fool who won't call her man."

Jeri blushes. "He's not my man," she corrects her friend.

Charmaine looks all indignant. "Well. That ain't my fault."

Jeri gives her a look. "I never said it was," she grumps.

"Are you on your period? Cause your PMS just 'bout hit me in my eye," Charmaine scolds.

Jeri wrinkles her nose. "I'm not even going to try to guess what that means."

Charmaine shakes her head and stands up. "It means what it means, girl. All your negativity done gave me a headache. I need some caffeine therapy." She points a finger at her. "You want anything from the coffee shop?"

Jeri shakes her head back and forth. "No, I do not. Thank you very much. They better give you frequent flyer miles down there. I swear you go there once a day."

Charmaine turns around. Her plaid, knit short-sleeved

sweater dress hits right above her knees. It peeks out above her bright pink leather boots that Jeri thinks make her look like an Easter egg. She points at Jeri. "I go there to get away from the office and little dark storm clouds, so mind your bizness, bee-yotch, and let me have my coffee."

Jeri feels bad. "It was just a joke, Charmaine. I'm sorry," she mumbles her apology.

Charmaine stares her down. "Mmm hmm. Now that's more like it," she says as she continues on her way.

"I could hang a hanger on that rack," the mailroom boy says as he enters the room with his head cranked in Charmaine's general direction.

"You want me to smack the stupid out of you now or later," Jeri threatens as she stands up from behind her desk.

Startled, he drops the fistful of letters. "I didn't see you..." he stutters as he shrinks beneath Jeri's glare. "I'm just gonna go now," he mutters as he backs out of the room with his mail cart. She squats down to gather the envelopes off the flat carpet. The fax machine starts up. She drops the pile of mail on her desk and stares at the fax. Julie's name is scrawled across the fax cover sheet. Jeri's heart races. "This is so dumb," she mutters, but she can't stop staring at the paper, waiting for the rest of it to print.

"It's unofficial, but I hear he was back at the bar the other night. I'm just trying to keep him out of trouble. He never answers his phone. If and when you get a hold of him, tell him once he's on probation he can't go to the bar, and he can't be drinking alcohol. Those are the rules, even if he is the Judge's friend! Thanks—Julie." Colon, line, dash, or eyes, mouth, tongue.

"Oh, boy. He's going to love hearing this," Jeri says as she whips out her phone and starts to text him but changes her mind. "Charmaine always says I never leave the office, so I guess I'll just have to prove her wrong," she says before checking her calendar. "I have nothing from now until five o'clock, and it's four o'clock now. Besides, I'm on salary, and there's plenty of days I've answered calls on the weekends," she reasons as she waltzes out the door, locking it behind her.

JERI:

Checking out early. Have a good weekend, Charmaine.

CHARMAINE:

This is about Caden.

JERI:

I never said that.

CHARMAINE:

You didn't have to. Purple emoji face with horns.

JERI: SHUT-UP.

I take it back. Don't have a nice weekend.

CHARMAINE:

Whatevs. I'll have a terrific weekend—esp now that I know you're chasin' Wolverine!

Jeri shoves her cell phone in her sweater pocket and climbs into her car. "I am not chasing anyone. I'm merely relaying a message in person to someone who doesn't answer his phone." She says as she starts her car. Jeri's phone rings. She sighs. "Hey, Mom," she answers through her steering wheel.

"Hello, daughter. What are you doing?"

"I'm driving," Jeri speaks into her steering wheel.

"But it's four o'clock. Why are you leaving work early? Is that a good idea?" her mom scolds.

"I work on salary, Mother," Jeri reminds her mom.

"Leaving work early is not a good habit," her mom scolds once more.

"Maybe I'll get fired, and then you won't have to worry about having a daughter who breaks people out of jail for a living," she suggests while holding in a giggle.

Her mom sighs. "I would ask you what you're doing, but now I'm afraid to."

"I'm going to see Caden," Jeri answers.

"I see," her mom says.

"What do you see?"

"Isn't that the name of the guy you bailed out two weeks ago?"

"Yeah," Jeri says. "But this is for work. I'm passing on a message from his P.O. officer," she says about the time she realizes how it sounds.

"Why are you doing it?"

"Because he doesn't answer his phone," Jeri supplies.

"That doesn't sound very responsible."

"He's a foreman at the salt mine, Mother. He's a very busy man."

"Too busy to answer to his probation officer? That's rather careless," her mother offers.

Jeri agrees with her mother, most of the time, but this is Caden, and she's sure he has a good reason. Maybe. Maybe she doesn't care. Maybe she's just happy to have a reason to see him in person again. That must be why the butterflies are going off in her stomach, no matter how hard her mother tries to silence them with her negativity. It's not her mother's fault. She tries to remind herself of that fact as she listens to her mother drone on about people making choices to end up where they are.

"Jeri?" her mother asks.

"Yeah, what?" Jeri says as she comes out of her daydream of seeing Caden one more time. "One more time," she mumbles.

"One more time what?" her mother asks.

"I don't know what I was saying," Jeri says. "What were we talking about?" she asks.

"Caden," her mother declares.

"No. Before Caden, what were we talking about?" Jeri asks, and it occurs to her that she's met the man who makes every other man she's ever met or dated pale in comparison.

"You left work early today," her mother supplies.

"Yes, but before that, Mom. What's going on with you?" Jeri says as she tries to get her mother onto another subject other than what Jeri seems to be doing wrong in her life—her work, her love interest—basically everything.

"My friends and I tried a new restaurant last week," her mom offers.

"Oh, that sounds fun. What was it?"

"It was like a sushi bar," her mom answers.

"And how did you like it?" Jeri asks.

"Well, I don't really care for uncooked meat, so..." her mother says. "And the Boba tea was so strong. You know I can't have that much caffeine. It makes me feel dizzy."

"What about vegetarian sushi," Jeri suggests. "There's no raw fish in there."

"Well, then I may as well eat white rice with green peas, and I can make that myself," her mother reasons.

"I don't know what to tell you, Mother," Jeri says. She feels like every discussion turns into some sort of argument. It's exhausting.

"Do you hear from Miles anymore?" her mother asks with a hopeful voice.

"Since I caught him in the mailroom with the temp and he shorted me on six months of rent?" Jeri says. "No. Not so much."

"Well, maybe what you think happened didn't," her mother says, and Jeri has to tell herself her mother thinks she's being helpful. "I mean, maybe it was good you caught them, so you could figure out what was wrong with your relationship."

"Why do you think his cheating is my fault?" Jeri hollers before she can stop herself.

"I didn't say that, darling," her mom says in a soothing voice that used to make Jeri feel better, but now it just pisses her off. "I'm just saying sometimes men need a variety. Did you ever try role-playing? I read about it in a magazine."

Jeri cringes at the thought and the fact that her mother suggested it. "I'm not having this conversation, Mother. My boyfriend cheated on me because he's a cheater. It had nothing to do with me, and if you read any articles that are like from the twentieth century, you would know that. Cheating isn't about the person they meet. It's about the game. It's about the secrets and the lies. It's about the fact that some people just aren't decent people," she rants, and then she stops. "I'm sorry. That wasn't meant for you. That was meant for Miles," Jeri offers.

Her mother clears her throat. "Well. With all of your strong opinions, no wonder Miles left you."

"For the last time, Mother. Miles didn't leave me," Jeri screams at her steering wheel. "I kicked him out," she yells.

I can see you're getting emotional, Jeri. That's not good for you, and it's not good for me either, so I'm just going to go now," her mother says, sounding all wounded. "Call me when you're feeling better."

Jeri stifles a groan. "Goodbye, Mother. I'm sorry I'm not feeling well," she mumbles right before she ends the call. She pulls into the parking lot and spots the guy she saw Caden talking to the one other time she was there. She rolls down her window and gives him a smile.

"Are you looking for Caden?" he asks.

"Yes," she says. "I have a letter for him."

"Give me a second," he says as he gets out his phone. "He should be at this address," he says as he shows her the text.

"Thanks," she says as she plugs it into her phone and backs out of the lot. "I'm doing Julie a favor," she says. "That's all this is."

Jeri is surprised to pull up to a funeral home. She thinks his co-worker pulled a trick on her, but then she spots his motorcycle. She's torn. She doesn't know what to do, and so she sits in her car staring at the front of the funeral home, feeling more foolish by the minute, but unable to leave. She scans the letter from Julie once more, trying to decide if it warrants borderline stalking someone at a funeral home. "Definitely not," she says as she rolls down the window because she's getting hot.

She starts to pull away from the curb but stops because a

line of people walks across the street up in front of her. She waits and tries to hide between the small space of her sun visor and the top of her steering wheel by ducking her head.

"Jeri?" his voice hits her ears, and she raises her head to see Caden standing across the street on the sidewalk in the middle of a bunch of people, waving madly at her.

Jeri stuffs the letter into her sweater pocket and opens her car door. She feels ridiculous as she crosses the street. "Hey, Caden," she says. "I didn't know what this address was," she says feeling more and more out of it the longer she talks, except for the smug smirk on his face that quickly wakes her from her stumbling and bumbling as she becomes more irritated by the fact that he's calling her out without saying a word.

A woman standing off to the side suddenly stands front and center. "Hello, I'm Maggie Brown. I'm Caden's mom."

Jeri almost chokes. "Hi, I'm Jeri. I'm..." She looks over at Caden for help.

"She's my bail bondsman," he supplies, "or should I say bail bondswoman?" he teases.

A man behind him slaps him hard on the back. "Caden, what a way to introduce a lovely young lady," he booms before sticking out his hand. Jeri lays her hand in his, and he swallows hers up, giving her a hard squeeze. "I'm Carl, Caden's old man." He looks her up and down, before giving her a big smile. "You sure are a tiny thing."

Jeri shifts her hand, gets a better grip, and gives his hand a squeeze. "I get the job done," she teases.

Carl takes his hand back, laughing as he does. "You're a firecracker," he booms. "I like you," he announces.

Maggie gives him a shove. "Don't mind, Carl. He's got a loud bark, but he's a teddy bear," she says with a wink.

Jeri looks past them at the funeral home. "I'm sorry for your loss, and I'm sorry to show up at an inopportune time."

Maggie slips an arm through Jeri's, surprising her as she leans in. "Don't you worry none. It was a visitation for our third cousin, Frank. He was eighty-five. He lived a good life. We're all getting ready to go down to the local bar and celebrate his life in one of his favorite places."

Jeri remembers Julie's letter. "That sounds very nice." She digs the paper from her pocket. "I'm just here to give this to Caden," she says as she looks up at him. "You can read it later," she starts, but Caden already has it open and unfolded.

Maggie sneaks a sideways look at Jeri and the way she looks at her son. She releases Jeri's arm and steps closer to her husband. "Come on, honey. I think the two of them have a few things to talk about," she says as she pulls him down the sidewalk.

Jeri watches the two of them walk away. She glances at Caden, who is still reading the letter. His face is blank. She wishes she knew what he was thinking. "So why didn't Julie bring me this letter?" he asks.

Jeri stands there beside him feeling inept. "She's very busy. There's two of us and one of her," she offers. "So sometimes we have more time than she does."

"Then why didn't Charmaine come?" he continues.

Jeri knows what he's after, but she's not about to admit it. "I guess I drew the short straw," she says. "Are you sorry it was me?" she teases, trying to flip the attention back on him.

He links his arm through hers, but there's nothing comforting about it, like his mother's was minutes ago. "I think we both know the answer to that," he says in more serious tone, sending the butterflies in her stomach into

123

hyperdrive. He gives her a tug. "So, are you walking with me to the bar or what?"

Jeri feels strange. "I don't know. I mean, not to be disrespectful, but I didn't know Frank."

Caden pats her arm. "Relax, Jeri. Frank never knew a stranger. In fact, I'd bet he'd be happy to know he's the reason I walk in with a beautiful woman on my arm," he teases.

Jeri giggles a little. "Your family is nothing like mine," she says.

Caden looks down at her. "Is that a good thing?"

She nods. "Yes, definitely." Her eyes drop to the sidewalk. "My mother would not approve of me going into a bar with a client," she adds in a quiet voice.

He pats the letter in his pocket. "Well, if it helps your case, given the contents of this letter, I think you better go in with me to keep a close eye on things. You can keep me out of trouble."

Jeri tenses beside him. "Is it going to be wild and crazy in there?"

Caden steps off the sidewalk into the grass. He pulls her halfway down the alley and opens a black door. "There's only one way to find out," he says as she gives her a gentle shove inside. Jeri's eyes adjust to the dim lighting. She's surprised to see wall-to-wall people standing around with drinks in their hands, chatting as they watch the slide show that fills up the back wall of the bar. Jeri stands close to Caden, who has a hand at the small of her back. The bartender smiles at him from behind the bar.

"Hey, Owen," Caden says. "I'll take a Bud Light."

Owen gives him a funny look. "How about her?" he asks as he glances in Jeri's direction.

Jeri leans toward Owen. "I'd like a lemonade."

"Plain?" Owen asks.

"No alcohol," she yells louder than necessary to be heard. Half the bar turns in her direction.

Owen laughs. "Got it," he says as he tosses a towel over his shoulder.

Jeri swallows hard while she wishes she were anywhere but where she's standing. She looks up at Caden. "Sorry," she mouths.

He takes a sip of his beer. "Don't be sorry for me. You're the one who's drinking lem-on-ade," he teases as he raises his glass high. "To Frank," he half-hollers to the crowd before they all do the same.

"To Frank," they answer before everyone takes a long drink. He turns back to Jeri. "Yep, it's a good thing you're here. I might need a ride home tonight."

Jeri makes a face of annoyance at him. "I'm not here to babysit you."

He takes another long drink before setting it down. Owen returns with another beer in one hand and Jeri's lemonade in the other.

"I'm here to deliver a letter, which I did, and that's it," she insists.

"You could have faxed that letter to my office," he fires back.

"I don't have your fax number," she argues.

"You could have called to get it," he says.

"You don't answer your phone," she points out.

"You're not going to admit you wanted to see me, are you?" he teases again.

She takes a drink of her lemonade. "You're not exactly hard to look at," she admits. She picks up his beer and takes a long drink of it. "I've seen worse views," she continues.

He takes her lemonade and takes a sip or two. "I could say the same," he says as he leans in closer.

Jeri hauls herself up on the barstool and leans back against the bar as she watches the slideshow of Frank's life on the far wall. She can't help but notice how every picture has groups of people in them, and they're all standing around smiling and laughing. She feels more than a little lonely when she thinks about her life. I'm plenty young, she thinks to herself. I've got time to spend with friends and family, but will I make a better effort she muses as she looks around the room. She takes in the groups clustered here and there, exchanging stories and laughter.

She turns back to Caden. She wonders how many people he knows here, and why he's standing beside her when he could be talking to them. She feels so out of place. She stands up. "I'm just going to go," she says.

He looks over at Owen as he picks up his beer. "I'm just going to step out a minute," he says as he follows her outside.

Jeri leans against the building. "I'm sorry, Caden. I shouldn't have come over today. I don't belong in there."

"Because it's a bar?"

Jeri shakes her head back and forth. "No, of course not."

"Because it's Frank's celebration of life?"

She nods her head. "Yes. Well, no. I don't know."

Caden stares down at her. "Just tell me what is bothering you."

"I don't belong here, in this town. I don't know anyone in there," she says as she tries to explain her feelings of inadequacy and loss for something she wants but knows she doesn't have. She feels selfish to think such things at someone else's celebration of life.

Caden shrugs his shoulders. "I do, and you're with me, so what's the big deal?"

"I'm not with you though," she insists, feeling more lost than ever. "I mean we're not together. I'm your bail bonds woman, Caden, so we can't be together," she reasons, and then she just feels stupid. "This was a terrible idea. I don't know what I was thinking, following you in there," she scolds, but she's mostly talking to herself.

Caden takes a sip of his beer. "If that's what bothering you, it doesn't bother me," he offers. "If you couldn't tell, my parents don't care." He says, but then he stops. "But your parents care," he says, testing the waters.

Jeri looks off toward the street as she leans on her hands. "I don't know...maybe," she says, feeling bad as she says it.

Caden takes another drink of beer. "Let me guess. They like someone more like Miles," he says, taking a shot in the dark.

Jeri can't believe how fast he pegged her family. "I don't know," she says as she stares at the ground. "Maybe," she all but whispers.

Caden nods his head. "I get it. I'm just a salt miner. I'm not good enough for you or them, but Miles, the fancy businessman with a college degree, is. It doesn't matter that he treated you like crap. That he lied to you," his voice raises just a little, and Jeri winces. He stops talking as soon as he sees the worry in her face. "I'm sorry. I didn't mean to upset you," he says as he steps closer, "but sooner or later you gotta decide whose life you're going to lead—yours or your mother's," he says in a low tone as he traces her collarbone with his fingertip. He looms over her as she leans against the wall. "I hope you choose me," he whispers in her ear.

She nods her head, but she won't look at him. "I know," she says, but he's not sure she means it, and this bothers him more than anything else.

She slips beneath his arm and inches away from him along the wall of the bar. "I gave you the letter. Please follow Julie's suggestions. I'm sorry, but I've got to go," she says as she turns and walks away from him.

eleven

Caden watches Jeri until she disappears from sight. He walks back inside with his drink that he sets down on the bar before he walks away from it and over to where his parents are. "Hey, Mom," he says.

She wraps her arm around her son's waist. "Caden." She looks around. "Where's Jeri? Did she go to the lady's room?" He tenses at her teasing, and she knows. "Oh. Did she have to leave early?"

"Somethin' like that," he mutters.

She looks up at her son. "Do you want to talk about it?"

He shrugs. "What's there to talk about? She doesn't think I'm worth it."

"Worth what?" Maggie asks, with a bit of concern. "It's just, I've never heard you sound so dejected."

"The fight, I guess, or whatever you want to call it," he says in an off-handed manner, but Maggie knows he's hurting.

"Come on, Caden. Take a walk with me," she prompts.

"Now?" he asks, "In the middle of Frank's party?"

Maggie gives him a pinch. "Yeah now. It's been three months since I've seen you. I don't know when I'll see you again. That mine keeps you pretty well tied up," she teases. Sort of.

"Hey. You and Dad raised me to be a hard worker," he grumps because he doesn't like feeling guilty, and his mom isn't wrong. He doesn't get home much.

"Yes, we did, and I'm real proud of you. You know that, but I miss seeing your handsome face," she says as she reaches up to squeeze his chin with her two fingers.

"Alright, Mom. Geez."

He follows her up the back stairway and out onto the balcony where she stands by the railing. "So do you think she's the one?" she asks.

Caden feels weird saying it out loud, but he can't lie to his mother. "Yes."

"Then what are you waiting for?" his mom demands.

"What do you mean?" he asks.

"Have you told her how you feel?" his mom asks.

"She knows I'm interested."

"And she's not?" his mom asks in a manner that implies she can't understand how anyone could not love her son. Caden can't help but smile.

"I think she is, and I usually have a pretty good read on women," he answers.

"Then what's the problem?" his mom asks.

"Between her job and the way we met, and the fact that her mother is still hung up on her cheatin' ex-boyfriend, Miles, it's fair to say her mother doesn't think I'm good enough for her daughter," he explains.

"Well, that's just stupid," Maggie states.

"That's what I said," he exclaims.

"Is this girl going to put on her grown-up pants and live her own life or her mother's?" his mom continues.

Caden leans on the railing and looks out at the street below. "I said that too," he agrees.

"You really are my son," his mom teases.

"I meant every word I said, but it wasn't enough to make her stay," Caden laments.

"You poor guy. You've never had a girl tell you no, have you?"

Caden turns to her with a tortured look on his face. "Don't make fun, Mom. This isn't funny." He rubs his chest. "It hurts."

She pats his hand. "I would never make fun. I'm sorry you're hurting. All I can say is if she means that much to you then don't give up so easily."

"What does that mean?" he asks. "What can I do if she doesn't want to see me?"

Maggie winks at her son and gives him an ornery smile. "I guess you find ways to *make* her see you," she says. "I'm sure you'll figure it out."

Caden tries to think, but it's hard. It's been a long week, and he's feeling butthurt from Jeri walking away from him. Again. "Are you sayin' I get myself thrown in jail again?" he asks his mom.

She snorts. "I wouldn't go that far," she quips. "Surely there are other ways you can see her. Find out what her interests are, what she spends time doing when she's not at work."

"How am I supposed to do that if she won't talk to me?" he asks.

Maggie rolls her eyes. "Look her up on Instagram or Twitter or Facebook."

Caden groans. "Wouldn't that make me a stalker?"

She gives him a shove. "No, son. That makes you attentive."

Caden pulls out his phone. He pulls up her website and hands it to his mother. "There. I looked up her work."

Maggie holds his phone out so she can see it without using her reading glasses. She laughs out loud. "That's adorable. I love it." She scrolls down the page, nodding. "Okay. She loves French bulldogs. She loves coasters, magnets, and coffee cups. She loves hot chocolate and a good book." His mom looks up from his phone. "This girl needs to get out more."

She studies him. "Think. Is there anything else she loves?"

He fidgets beneath his mother's stare. "She loves her Uncle Saul," he suggests. "She loves Freebirds," he adds when he thinks of her boots.

"Ooh, those are some high-dollar boots," Maggie exclaims.

"She wears them like every day," he adds in a defensive tone.

Maggie raises her hands in surrender. "Nothin' wrong with good taste, son. Calm down." She hands his phone over. "You got anything else?"

He shrugs. "She likes to chase after me," he says with an ornery grin, "but once she catches up to me, she runs away."

His mom snaps her fingers. "Maybe we can work with that," she says as her eyes light up. "Tell me more about the chase," she requests.

"Well, the first time she tracked me down was because I called the Judge and told him I couldn't make the court date, but I didn't tell her, and so she drove over here from the city.

I wasn't at the courthouse where I was supposed to be. That really ticked her off. She drove clean out to the worksite just to chew me out," he explains. "And then I guess today she all but volunteered to bring me an unofficial letter from the P.O. officer as a favor, or so she said. For a while she was friendly and receptive but then somethin' just flipped a switch, and she took off on me," he muses. "She started talkin' about how she didn't belong here, that I knew everyone, and she didn't know anyone. I told her that she was with me, and everythin' was fine, but she snuck outside. So I followed her. We talked long enough for me to figure out her parents don't like how we met, what I do for a livin', and that they still like her ex-boyfriend who cheated on her."

His mom waves her hand. "Forget about her parents. You can't do anything about them. If they choose to like someone who cheated on their daughter, I'm not sure what that says about their marriage or how they feel about how someone treats Jeri," she reasons.

She claps her hands. "Let's focus on Jeri."

"And her Uncle Saul. He likes me," Caden adds.

Maggie's ears perk up. "How do you know that?"

"I've met him. I've been to his apartment. I help him put his cathouse together for his cats."

Maggie shoves him. "That changes everything. Why didn't you say that in the beginning?"

"I didn't know it mattered," he grumbles.

"Of course, it matters. If he likes you, I'd bet he'd be willing to help you find ways to spend time with Jeri," she says.

"You think I should tell him I'm chasin' his niece," Caden states.

"As long as your intentions are honorable, yes," his

mother explains. She nudges his ribs with her elbow. "Your intentions are honorable, are they not?"

"Seriously, Mother. This isn't old England. I'm not Mr. Darcy, and she's not Elizabeth Bennett," he grumbles.

"I didn't know you watched my favorite movie," she exclaims.

"I can't not watch it when you watch it obsessively," he growls.

"It's a great movie," she insists. "Anyway, I don't know. You're both pretty stubborn, and it sounds to me like your pride might be getting in the way of a meaningful relationship."

Caden stares down at his empty phone screen, wishing she would text him. "I think I'm gonna call it a night," he says. "See ya later, Mom."

"I love you," she says.

"I love you too," he answers.

Caden thinks of the slide show and the words Jeri said to him as she leaned against the wall. Now that he thinks about it, she looked so trapped and alone. Caden mulls this over as he drives home. An idea comes to him.

It's been forever since he's been on a road trip. He can't think of a better way to get to know someone by taking a long drive together. He gets to work on his plan by digging through all the closets in his apartment for picnic items.

Caden falls asleep with Jeri on his mind. He hopes she enjoys being spontaneous. He wakes bright and early, ready for a new day and a new start that has him knocking on her door at eight AM, setting off a couple of barking dogs. A bleary-eyed Jeri opens the door in a tee shirt and cotton shorts. Her shoulder-length blonde hair dances in the slight breeze that comes up behind him. She shivers and steps off to the side to mostly hide behind her door. Caden doesn't know what to do. She hasn't said a word. She gestures with her hand. "Are you coming in or what?"

Caden steps inside. He's already feeling foolish. His excitement over the road trip dissipates quickly. "I thought maybe we could go on a day trip."

Jeri looks startled. "Where do you thinking we are going?"

"I don't know. Where would you like to go?" he asks in a brighter tone than he feels, especially when she's scowling at him.

She tosses a hand on her hip. "You drive over here on a Saturday, wake me up, tell me you want to go on a road trip, but you don't know where," she states as if it is the most idiotic plan in the world.

He shrugs. "I didn't want to come off like some male chauvinist," he says. "You know, like one of those guys who takes a girl to a restaurant and then proceeds to order her food for her as if she's incapable of her own thoughts."

Jeri crosses her arms on her chest. "What if I don't want to go anywhere?"

"How about a movie day?" he asks in the most pleasant voice he can manage. Ever since he thought up the road trip idea, he's kind of anxious to go.

She taps her fingers on her chin. "My movie days are usually spent alone. I like to gather up my favorite treats and my babies and veg out on chic flicks all day." She gives him an ornery grin. "Does that sound like fun to you?"

Caden fights his initial reaction, which is to groan at the sound of the term *chic flick*. "I'll admit it's not my favorite idea, but maybe we could squeeze like a few action movies in there? Like what if it's an action-packed rom-com like *Mr. and Mrs. Smith*?"

Jeri wrinkles her nose. "Too intense and forced. It's completely unnatural. If I'm going to watch a movie like that it may as well be *Salt* or *Jason Bourne*, but only if Matt Damon is the main character."

"What about a good old classic like *The Sandlot*?"

"Isn't that like a kid's movie?" she teases.

"I don't think so," he says as he tilts his head to the side. "No. Definitely not. It covers baseball, procreation, suspense, CUJO-like dogs, sexism, and racism." He shakes his head. "Definitely not just a kid's movie."

Jeri can't believe how much her sour mood has improved since he walked through her door. She is not a morning person. "If I go on a day trip with you, how are we traveling, because I am not getting on the back of that bike of yours. It's a deathtrap."

Caden looks all offended. "It's perfectly safe. I'm an excellent driver. I have two helmets," he offers.

The look on her face tells him she's not buying anything he's selling. "My Uncle Charlie is a Vietnam veteran. He was shot down *two times* in the war," she holds up two fingers for emphasis. "If he says motorcycles are dangerous deathtraps, that's good enough for me," she declares. "I'm not riding on your bike."

He gives her most charming smile. "How do you feel about drivin' your car?"

She gives him a little shove. "You have a lot of nerve, mister. Telling me we're going on a day trip, and then asking me to be the driver." Jeri can't believe how good of a mood she's suddenly in as she points to the keys hanging on the hook in the kitchen on the wall. "Wherever we go, you're driving."

She grabs a hold of his arm and starts tugging on him.

"What are you doin' now?" he asks.

"I'm going to go take a shower and get ready. You're coming in the kitchen and showing me what you can cook for breakfast."

Caden has a moment of panic. "You want me to go through your fridge and make you breakfast?"

She laughs at the tone of his voice. "Yep. I'm not going anywhere until I eat something, and since you're taking over my Saturday, the least you can do is make me some breakfast." She starts to leave the room but turns back around. "And cold breakfast in a bowl with milk doesn't count."

He opens her fridge. He starts to panic when he sees a bunch of bags of lettuce and all different sorts of cheeses. "Where's the meat?" he says as he checks every shelf and drawer. "Please don't tell me she's a vegetarian," he mutters. He moves on to the freezer. "Salmon," he says as he wrinkles his nose, but then he remembers the Worcestershire sauce. "Improvise. You can do this," he says as he recalls a coffee shop breakfast he had the last time he traveled.

He turns on the oven, takes out the salmon filet and puts it in a bowl of warm water while he waits for the oven to heat to 325. He smiles at Jeri's three choices of half loaves of bread. "Aha. You're a multi-grain with nuts kind of girl." He checks her windowsill and is happy to find an avocado sitting there. "Now we're talking," he mutters before returning to the fridge to get out the eggs. He cracks a few and separates them into two different bowls. He opens the bottom drawer once more and snatches up a few oranges.

Twenty-eight minutes later, Jeri walks into the kitchen.

She's surprised to find two pieces of wheat toast covered with mashed avocado. Orange slices are lined up neatly on top of that. Brown sauce zig-zags across the oranges and the half salmon filet sitting atop an egg white accompanying the toast like a sidecar. She raises an eyebrow at Caden who sits across from her at the kitchen table.

"Breakfast is served," he says as he holds his breath.

She raises an eyebrow. "I have to say, you surprise me. This is impressive." She gives him a small grin. "I love all the color."

He clears his throat. "I have a confession to make. I didn't think of this on my own. I ate something like this once at a coffee shop. I wasn't sure about it when I read it on the board, but I decided to try it, and it was really good."

She picks up her piece of toast. "Shall we?" He does the same. They bump their pieces of bread against each other. "Here's to trying new things," she says before she takes a big bite of toast, avocado, and orange.

The two of them sit in their chairs, chewing in silence. She takes a drink of water. "I think maybe it's an acquired taste," she suggests.

He coughs a little before he takes a big drink of water. "I thought the sweetness of the orange would offset the Worcestershire sauce, but I may have put a little too much sauce on there."

"Maybe try some of the salmon and egg white," she suggests. "It's probably more bland."

They both take a bite of salmon and egg. He wrinkles his nose again. "Well, that might have been on epic fail."

Jeri gets up and gets in the fridge. She returns with big bottle of Ranch. She sets it down on the table with a flourish. "Here. Try some of this."

"It's Ranch dressing," he says with confusion in his voice. "You eat this for breakfast?"

She shrugs. "It goes with a lot of things, and it usually makes them better," she says as she pours some on her plate. She dips her toast in it before taking another bite. She makes a silly face at him with a mouthful of food.

Caden picks up the Ranch. "I guess," he mutters as he squirts a little on the side. They finish their breakfast with the help of Butch and Sundance who sit dutifully at their feet licking their chops waiting for the next bite. Jeri laughs when Butch spits out the orange slice, peel and all. She scoops it up with her napkin and tosses them both in the trash.

"How do you feel about a few extra travelers on this road trip of ours?" she asks while pointing at her dogs.

Caden loves her silliness. He can't believe how relaxed it is between them. He's not sure when it changed, but he knows he likes it. "It's your car."

She nods her head. "This is true." She takes a deep breath. "Should we ask Uncle Saul to come along?"

Caden feels like his plan for alone time with Jeri is slipping away from him, but his mom's question rings in his ears, particularly the one where she asked him how bad he wants to spend time with Jeri. He knows the answer to that. He'll take any time she's willing to give him. "Sure, if you think he'd want to."

Jeri gives him an ornery look and throws her hands in the air before hopping out of her chair. "Hey. I'm just taking a page out of your book," she says as she does a little side-to-side bounce, waving her arms about as if she's using them for balance. "I'm goin' with the flow, feelin' easy and free," she says as she does a silly twirl with her hands over her head. Her signature sweater slides away from her raised wrists towards her elbows. Her long skirt swooshes around her.

"Easy there, tiger. Don't trip on your skirt," he teases. "Don't you give those things a break on the weekends?" he adds.

"Excuse me?" she asks.

"Your skirts," he says as he points.

"Fine," she grumps. "I'll go change."

Caden sits on the couch. Butch and Sundance soon jump on the couch beside him. They stare up at him as if they're expecting him to do something. "What?" he says to the two of them. "What's you guys' deal?"

He turns toward the sound of footsteps. Caden is floored to see Jeri's blonde hair hanging loose in a ponytail. There's something about the swish-swish of her hair going back-and-forth that makes him a little crazy. "Is that a U of M sweatshirt?" he asks as he takes in her capri pants and some sort of sockless shoe.

She coughs. "Yes, it is, but if you give me grief about it, I'm putting my prairie back on," she warns.

He raises his hands in surrender. "Chillax, girl. I didn't say anythin' negative. I like it," he says with a small smirk. "That's all."

She makes a kissing sound for her dogs, but it's Caden who jumps at the sound. She claps her hands. "Come on, Butch and Sundance, let's go," she orders.

———

Before too long they pull up to Saul's apartment. She turns to Caden who sits in the driver's seat of her Spark car. "Would it be alright if I go in alone?"

He's confused because he felt like he and Saul got along really well the last time they met, but he's not about to start an argument with her for no good reason. "Sure," he answers.

Minutes later, Jeri and Saul come down the sidewalk. Saul is styling in his khakis, button-up shirt, cardigan sweater, and a bowtie. His dark green beret sits rakishly to the side. He tips the front of it as he approaches the Spark car before he climbs in the back with Butch and Sundance. "You might be a little overdressed for what we have planned, Saul. I hope you're not disappointed," Caden says by way of an apology.

Saul reaches over the front seat and gives his shoulder a hard squeeze. "Nonsense, son. Any time I leave the house for a social visit is reason to celebrate. I like to look sharp. You never know who you might meet."

twelve

Jeri can't believe how much it doesn't bother her that the day is not going at all how she expected. Caden was the last person she thought she'd see on her doorstep so early on a Saturday, especially since he seemed to avoid her from the beginning. And then she made such a fool of herself at the bar the other night. She turns to look at her uncle sitting in the backseat with Butch and Sundance. His whole face is lit up as he stares out the window. This makes her so happy.

Caden looks in the rearview mirror. "Hey, Saul," he calls out.

"Yeah?" Saul replies.

"Where should we go?" Caden asks.

Saul leans back in the seat. "You asking me where you should go, or where I would like to go?" he teases.

Caden laughs out loud. "Where would you like to go, Saul?"

Jeri waits for Saul's answer. She has no idea what he's going to say.

"How do you feel about museums?"

Jeri holds in a groan. Museums are not her favorite.

"They're alright," Caden blurts out. His deep voice fills the confines of her tiny car.

"Have you been to the submarine museum?" Saul asks.

"No, I haven't," Caden says as he turns towards Jeri. "Have you been?" he asks her.

Jeri feels claustrophobic just thinking about walking inside a submarine. "I could take the dogs for a walk while you two go in," she offers, hoping Caden won't protest her suggestion.

"Okay," he says in a quieter tone that sounds a little disappointed, but he pastes a smile on his face as he looks back at Saul in the mirror. "Do you know how to get to this museum?"

Saul taps his fingers on the seat. "I think it's in a few towns over," he muses before poking Jeri in the shoulder with his index finger. "Can't you google it in your phone?"

Jeri leans away from his poking finger. "Give me a minute, please."

The car is quiet as she types in *submarine museums near me*, thinking Saul's probably mistaken. She's pretty sure there's no such thing as a museum inside a submarine or that they're anywhere near it. She's surprised when it pops up on her screen. "It says it's eighty miles from here," she says as she turns to Caden. "Is that okay?"

He points at her dash. "This says little Sparky here can go another 123 miles before we have to gas up, so I'd say we're fine there."

Caden looks at Saul in the rearview mirror once more. "So tell me, Saul. Were you ever married?"

Saul nods his head. "I sure was. Her name was Goldie.

We were married fifty-seven years. She was the love of my life," he says as solemn as a vow.

"How did you meet?" Caden prompts.

Saul grins. "Well, it's kind of a funny story. I was engaged to a girl named Sally."

Jeri turns toward her uncle. "What? I've never heard this story before."

Saul gives her an ornery look. "That's because you've never asked."

Caden smirks at Jeri and pokes her in the knee. "Guess he told you," he teases.

Jeri swats his hand away. "Go on, Uncle Saul. Tell me more."

"I grew up in a small town, the kind where we all knew each other. We all went to the same small-town high school. Many of us married our high school sweethearts. Sally was a girl I dated all through school. She was a pretty girl. She was a good cook. She was sweet. She loved her parents."

He pauses. Jeri is confused. "What was wrong with her?"

Saul chuckles. "Nothing. There was nothing wrong with her. It was me," he offers. "I didn't know what I wanted, except that I knew I couldn't stay in that small town after I turned eighteen."

Jeri frowns. "But you spent most of your life in a suburb, which is kind of the same as living in a small town," she argues.

Saul nods his head. "You're right, and I suppose it doesn't make sense, but I just felt like I had to get out of the town I grew up in, or I would never know who I was meant to be."

"I think you're saying you felt like everyone had this picture of who you were, and you felt like you didn't fit in their frame," he suggests.

Saul points toward the rearview mirror. "Exactly." He leans up a little so he's more between them. "I don't think they meant to hold me back. But I just had this feeling I could be more than what they expected of me."

Jeri considers the job she's in. "I think I get it. I mean, I love my job, but it's the sort of job that I'm not sure I want to go to my next class reunion and talk about, even though it's never failed to pay the bills."

"Are you saying you're not jumpin' at the chance to tell all your old buddies from high-school your job is bailin' people out of jail?" Caden teases.

Jeri bristles. "Whatever. I bailed your butt out of jail."

Caden raises his eyebrows at her. "I know, and I can't say I'm sorry about it." He gives her a wink. "I wouldn't get myself thrown in jail for just anyone," he teases.

She gives him a playful shove. "Whatever. You didn't know me when they locked you up."

He gives her another grin. "I'd get thrown in there again for you."

Jeri isn't sure how to respond to Caden's flirting. It almost seems as if he means what he's saying. She feels relieved when she sees Saul sitting back in his seat. She needs a subject change. "Excuse us, Uncle Saul. You didn't finish your story. How did you meet your wife?"

Saul taps his hands on his knees. "Well, I was eighteen years old in 1958. I had everything I thought I needed packed into the suitcase my parents bought to send me off to college with."

"Something else you didn't do, I'm guessin'," Caden states.

"You are very astute," he growls. "Can I go on with my story?" he asks with some warning in his tone.

"Yes," Caden replies meekly, like a reprimanded child.

"My parents and I had just had it out for the last time about my future. I wanted to join the Army. They wanted me to go to college. I told them I could pay my own way. They couldn't figure out why I wasn't more grateful for them offering to take care of my tuition. So twelve days after I graduated, I packed up my suitcase and started walking."

Jeri can't believe what she's hearing. "You hitchhiked?"

"I did. The car I drove all through high school was my dad's. He told me I could have it if I went to college. When I refused to go where he wanted, he took his car back. He told me if I wasn't ready to listen to reason or get a free education, I could make my own way in the world." He sighs. "And so I did, and that's when I met Goldie," he laughs. "She was sparkly and flashy as her first name. I was walking down the highway about five miles outside of my hometown when a long, green Impala pulled up next to me. A girl with blonde shiny hair, the shiniest I'd ever seen, leaned out of the car window. Her hair fell in waves around her face. It made her look like an angel. She tipped her head sideways, and our eyes met. She had the greenest eyes. They looked like emeralds. And that smile. There was just something about the curve of her lips that turned me on my ear, and she was looking at me," he states. Even though he's talking to the two of them, it's almost as if he's talking to himself.

"Was she driving?" Jeri asks.

"No," Saul answers quickly. "Her boyfriend was."

Jeri's jaw drops. "She had a boyfriend when you met?"

"I don't know, Saul. Your meet-cute sounds a little scandalous," Caden says as he winks at Jeri. By the grumpy look on her face, she doesn't find it very funny.

Jeri turns back to her uncle. "So what happened next?"

Saul studies his niece. "Well, it didn't start out as a fairytale, but we got our fairytale ending," he says with a satisfied grin that tells Jeri he knows she's not going to accept that as the rest of the story. She doesn't.

"Tell me what happened with the guy," she prods.

Saul chuckles. "Alright, fine. It's not exactly my proudest moment," he says, but he doesn't sound too sorry about it. "So I get in the car, and we aren't very far down the road when I realize he's a bit of a blockhead. He was a looker. There's no arguing that. They made a very handsome couple."

Caden gives him a funny look in the mirror.

Saul goes on. "Well, they did. He seemed nice enough, but the longer I talked to him, I didn't think he was the type of guy who would keep her interested. He wasn't much for conversation," he explains.

"You could talk the hind leg off a dog," Jeri rattles off, using one of her uncle's favorite idioms.

"That's fair," Saul answers. "So anyway, somewhere during our drive to the next big city with an Army base he was going to leave me at, I talked him into joining the Army."

Caden shakes his head. "No way. You were going to join the Army, and he was going to get the girl. You flipped the story."

Saul nods his head. "I did. It was so easy it wasn't funny. All I had to do was convince him I didn't think he was man enough to join the Army, and that's all it took. He joined up just to prove me wrong."

"But you didn't join," Jeri muses.

"Not after I met Goldie. No, ma'am. She was the kind of girl you'd leave a country for," Saul swears.

"But you didn't leave a country, Uncle. You stayed in the country," Jeri argues.

"Same difference, girl. The point is I thought I needed adventure, but then I met her. It turns out she was my greatest adventure," he says the last eight words in a quieter voice.

Jeri's throat tightens. Her eyes water. She feels ridiculous, but she can't stop it. She wonders if anyone will ever come close to feeling that way about her. Then she feels selfish for thinking that. "That was the sweetest story I've ever heard," she says to her uncle.

"Saul left his fiancée, and then he stole Goldie away from someone else, and you think that's sweet," Caden protests before checking his rearview mirror. "Sorry, Saul. I'm just sayin'."

Saul flips Caden a what-you-gonna-do-about-it look in the mirror. "If you're waiting for me to apologize, don't hold your breath," Saul drawls. "Goldie wasn't married when we met. We had a wonderful marriage. She was the love of my life, and I don't regret a single day I spent with her."

Caden glances at Jeri, and he feels itchy. He thinks he might understand what Saul is talking about, and it scares him. "How much longer do we go down this road," he asks her. Not because he wants to know, so much as he needs to change the subject.

"As far as we need to go," she responds. He feels like she's saying something else.

"If that's what you want," he replies.

She looks confused at his words, and she holds up her phone. "I think my phone is frozen. I'm waiting for it to tell me how many miles before our next turn."

"Oh, right," he says. He's embarrassed. He can't believe he misread her so badly.

"Hey. Can we pull into that gas station?" Saul asks as he stretches his long arm between the two of them to point out the front windshield.

Minutes later, Caden pulls into the parking lot. Jeri hops out first and shuts her door. Caden starts to follow, but Saul grabs a hold of his arm. "Don't rush her, boy. Let her come to you. She's a stubborn one. If she thinks you're trying to force her into something she's going to turn tail and run fifty miles in the other direction."

Caden swallows hard. He can't believe he's taking advice from an eighty-five-year-old man. But Saul did steal someone's girl back in the day, *and* he's her uncle. He seems to know her pretty well. "Her parents don't like me. They don't think I'm good enough for her."

Saul laughs out loud again. "There's loads of people who aren't good enough for that spoiled baby brother of mine. My hard-earned money put that snot-nosed brat through college, but do you think he ever said thank you? Did he ever pay it back? To hear him tell it he's earned every penny he has, and he has a lot of pennies," he bellows. "But he sure has a sweetheart of a daughter. I love Jeri like she's one of my own." He slaps Caden's shoulder. "I wouldn't worry a bit about getting her parent's approval. They don't like her career choice either. If she were my daughter, I'd be proud of her. She's a hard worker. She's a kind person. She has a good heart. That's good enough for me," he says. "If you know what's good for you, she's good enough for you too." He opens his door and puts a foot on the ground. "C'mon. Let's get in there before she comes lookin' for us."

Caden glances at Butch and Sundance. "You go ahead. I'll leash up the little monsters and walk them around a bit."

Saul moves past him. "You're a good man, Caden Brown," he calls as he walks away.

Jeri sneaks around her uncle on the way back to the car. "Did I hear someone accusing you of being a good man?" she teases as she reaches for the leashes.

He hands them over. Their hands brush, and it's electric. She keeps an eye on her dogs and avoids making eye contact with Caden.

"Thanks. I'll finish walking them. You can go inside." Her voice is tight and stiff, but he knows what he feels and what he saw. There was surprise in her eyes. Heightened awareness lingers between them. He wants to grab a hold of it, but she's running away.

Saul's words of warning burn Caden's ears. He's not wrong. She is stubborn and headstrong. There's no forcing her to acknowledge her feelings. It's about to drive him crazy, but he can wait. The harder the fight the sweeter the surrender, he decides. Caden catches Saul at the counter buying junk food he's pretty sure Jeri wouldn't approve of for a man his age. He grins and keeps on walking. He's her uncle, Caden reminds himself. Saul's diet or lack of it isn't his problem. Minutes later, Caden finds himself at the same counter, somehow spending thirty-seven dollars. He walks out with two bags of goodies that he tosses at Jeri's feet right before he turns the car on.

"What's this?" she says as she digs through the plastic bags. "Good grief, Caden. Did you buy *anything* healthy?"

He shakes his fountain drink in her ear. "You can have my ice cubes," he teases.

"Lighten up, Jeri," Saul grumps from the backseat. "What's a road trip without some snack food?"

"Yeah, Jeri," Caden agrees. "Give me something salty to commemorate our first road trip together," he teases.

She opens the peanut-butter-filled pretzels. "Here, have some protein with a side of carbs and about ten grams of sodium," she says as she hands him a handful of pretzel squares.

Caden pops a couple in his mouth and crunches. "Nah. I'd say that's more like four grams of sodium," he jokes.

"Enjoy worry-free eating while you're young," she complains.

"You sayin' you're an old lady?" he fires back.

"She may not be old, but she dresses like an octogenarian," Saul says. "She eats like an old lady, and she worries like an old lady," her uncle declares.

"Stop ganging up on me," Jeri protests. Her voice is a little shaky. Although he feels they speak the truth, Caden feels bad.

"Calm down, Jeri. We're just playin'."

"At my expense," she insists.

"What do we know?" Saul chimes in. "We're just a couple of nerds driving a few hours down the road to see a submarine museum."

"And it's going to be awe-some," Caden adds in a voice of reverence that says he means every word.

Jeri is upset at Caden's teasing, but she can't help but love how wonderful he's been with all the extra guests she invited along for the day.

"You're right. It's going to be pretty cool," she agrees. "Be sure and take lots of pics for me, please."

Saul leans up between them again. "So, Caden," he booms. "How is a guy like you not married?"

Caden almost chokes on his pretzel piece at Saul's unexpected question. By the look in Saul's eye in the mirror, it's evident Saul knows exactly what he's doing—making Caden as uncomfortable as possible.

"I guess I haven't met the right one yet," he grounds out.

"Well, that's a shame," Saul answers.

"That someone hasn't scooped me up yet?" Caden asks. "I know. I'm quite the catch."

"So you keep insinuating, but that remains to be seen," Jeri responds.

"Ouch. That was hurtful," Caden pretends to be offended, but she knows better.

"Yeah, okay."

"You think you can't hurt my feelings?" he questions her.

"I think it'd take a lot," she replies.

"Hey," Saul hollers, making them both jump. "You two knock it off. I ain't listenin' to this bickerin' all the way to the museum. If you can't be nice to each other, then take me home."

Jeri looks confused. "This is how we communicate," she says.

"I don't like it," Saul argues.

"What are you going to do if we can't stop?" Jeri asks in earnest.

"I'm going to hitchhike back home. I've done it before," he promises.

"I don't think there are any Goldies waitin' to pick you up and take you home today, Saul," Caden teases. "At least not ones your age. They're probably playin' bridge or gettin' their hair done."

Jeri frowns at him. "Are you saying elderly women don't have anything better to do?"

"Not necessarily. Who says I don't want to play bridge someday or spend half the day sitting under a hair dryer? Do you know how relaxin' it is to have someone else wash your hair?" Caden jokes.

"You have an answer for everything, don't you?" Jeri accuses.

"Alright, alright. Shut up already," Saul scolds.

"Gladly," Caden answers.

"Yeah," Jeri agrees.

"But I said it first," Caden points out.

"What you want? A medal?" she demands.

"Why are you still talking? You said you would be quiet," Saul grumbles.

"He always has to have the last word," Jeri whines.

"So do you," Caden replies.

"You just don't like it 'cause I'm a woman," she goes on.

"I'm very aware you're a woman, and I can't say that I mind it one bit. That's not the problem," Caden suggests.

"Then what is the problem?" she demands.

"There's somethin' between us, and you're ignorin' it. I want to know why."

"If there was something, and I'm not saying there is, you know why. It starts with the fact that we met when you were in jail," she exclaims. "Not to mention you're not the easiest guy to get a hold of or get along with. You're arrogant and rude. You never show up on time to appointments. You can't give me one common courtesy call. You're as stubborn as a mule. You have a terrible sense of style."

"Do you realize how superficial you sound?" he scolds.

"And yet you're still interested," she says.

"Trust me. I'm gettin' less and less interested the more you talk," he vows.

Jeri's jaw drops. "That was cold."

"I don't see you shiverin'," he threatens.

"Just forget it," Saul calls out from the backseat.

They both turn back to face him. "What's that?" Jeri asks her uncle.

"I said, forget it. I don't want to go anywhere with either one of you," he scolds. "You're a couple of clucking hens. You're both so busy squawking at each other and throwing up dirt with your little digs that you forget what's important," he growls.

"I'm sorry, Saul. I would be more cordial, but she..." Caden says before he's cut off.

"Cordial? What kind of word is that? What are you like stuck in the early 1800s? *Lord Brown* from the House of Salt," she taunts.

"No, I'm not," he says before he gives her a short stare. "I was merely pointin' out you're not the only one who has a brain or an extensive vocabulary," he declares. "*Moreover*, the reason we don't get along is because tryin' to get close to you is like tryin' to hug a porcupine. You spit out barbs like they're little quills flyin' through the air to pierce the skin of anyone who tries to get to know you."

"I'm a professional, Caden. I take my job seriously. Something you've yet to exhibit," she remarks in a tone that can only be known as scathing.

"I risked my life goin' into that mine," he bellows. "You know. You were there." He sighs heavily. "If that's not dedication, I don't know what is."

"Turn on the radio," Saul demands.

"Gladly," Caden agrees as he reaches for the tiny knob, but she beats him to it.

"This is my car," she tells him as he gives her a look.

"But I'm driving," he argues.

She turns up the country music station. "How's that, Uncle Saul?" she asks, but he doesn't answer.

They drive on in silence for the next ten minutes. "In case either of you are wondering, you missed your turn about seven miles back," Saul drawls from the backseat.

"Why didn't you say something?" Jeri asks, but she's pretty sure she knows the answer.

"Would you have heard me?" he states.

Caden taps the brakes, signals right, and pulls off the long stretch of highway abruptly. "What are you doing? Trying to ruin my car? It isn't made for this type of driving. It's not a motorcycle," she scolds.

He whips his head sideways to face her. "You want to drive?"

She stares out her window. "You're the one who wanted to go on a road trip," she mutters out the side of her mouth. He ignores her as he looks both ways a few times before doing a U-turn in the middle of the highway.

"You can't do that. It's against the law," she says.

"Well, I just did. I'm not drivin' seventeen miles down the road just to turn around," he reasons.

"You're breaking the law," she continues. "I don't know why I'm surprised."

"Which way am I goin' next?" he asks Saul in the rearview mirror.

"Ask Jeri," Saul says stubbornly.

She turns to look at him. "You're the one who said we missed our turn."

Saul points at her phone. "You're the one with the directions."

"Fine," she relents. "You're going to go west on Highway sixty-three for the next twenty-eight miles."

"And then what?" he asks.

"Don't worry about it. Let's just see if you can do that much," she comments.

"I think I know how to drive down a road," Caden grumbles.

"That remains to be seen," she grumbles right back.

"What's that supposed to mean? We're halfway there, aren't we?" he answers.

"You flipped a Uey in the middle of a major highway because you missed your turn," she says as she waves her hands all around. "If Uncle Saul hadn't told you, you would've kept going in the wrong direction."

He opens his mouth to argue for the hundredth time, but he catches Saul's look of warning in the rearview mirror. Caden mentally counts to ten in his mind. Twice.

"Well?" she commands.

He turns to look at her. He can't believe all he wants to do is kiss her senseless. All they've been doing for the past thirty minutes is argue. "It's not about the destination, darlin'. It's about the journey," he says as he wills her to give him a break and have a sense of humor.

"Says a man who won't admit he's going in the wrong direction," she states in a tone so full of self-confidence he can't help but admire her.

"If the direction I'm goin' leads me to you, it ain't wrong," he continues.

"You think you're so smooth just because you've got an

156

answer for everything," she argues, but her voice is quiet. He senses her resistance is weakening.

"I try," he drawls.

He looks in the mirror once more. "So, Saul, did Sally's parents forgive you for dumping their daughter?"

"Not at first, they didn't. Eventually she married a local dentist. After that, they forgot about being mad at me," he says with a chuckle. "Goldie's parents weren't too wild about me either, not when we first got together."

"Why's that?" Caden asks.

"Well, they liked her first boyfriend, the one who joined the Army. And when he joined the Army and I didn't, that made them like him even more, what with him being patriotic and all," he adds.

"So you never joined?" Jeri says.

"No. I never did. Goldie and I spent a few years on the road, traveling. We spent many nights on the road, sleeping beneath the stars," he daydreams. "It was wonderful."

"Wait a minute. How'd you do that if you didn't have a car?" Caden interrupts.

"She had a car. That Impala was hers, and it was one hot car," he says. "It was a two-door hard-top convertible."

"Suh-weet," Caden acknowledges.

"It was just a car," Jeri says.

Saul shakes his head back and forth. "Y'all don't know the magic of a backseat," he muses.

Caden cracks up a little. "I'm sorry. It's just the words you used."

Saul's eyes twinkle with delight. "That's not what I'm talking about, although those are great memories too, but that's between me and my wife." He leans back and looks at the ceiling before closing his eyes. "I'm talking about sitting in a seat long enough to stretch your legs and wide enough to have your girl sitting right next to you, curling into your side as you lean against the cool leather and look out the panoramic back window at the stars. The window behind you is rolled down just enough to let a cool breeze in along with the nighttime sounds of the crickets chirp, and the bullfrogs croak. It's every country road you've been down and every one you haven't seen. It's a different kind of peace and quiet. It's feeling settled and content because of the person next to you and the perfection of uninterrupted nature," he explains to a car that's quieter than it has been since it sat empty in Jeri's driveway that morning.

Caden and Jeri look at each other in awkward silence before they return to staring straight ahead.

"So after the twenty-eight miles, you're going to go north on Highway twenty-three for like seven miles, and then you'll turn right on Road X and go like six miles before you get to the town of Silverton, and that's where the submarine museum is," Jeri says.

"Thank you," Caden replies. "Could you snapshot it though, because I don't know if I'll remember all that."

"Sure," she says as she pushes on both sides of her phone and holds the screen closer to his face. "Got it," she says in a happier, more pleasant tone.

Saul smiles as he watches the two of them talking.

Caden catches the satisfied look on Saul's face but pretends he doesn't, just like he works extra hard at not looking the same way as Jeri sneaks looks in his direction. Caden hopes she's thinking about what Saul said because he is. He wasn't just playing around when he told her it was about the journey and not the destination and who you take the journey with.

Caden's thinking about these things when she taps him on the knee. "Better slow down. Your turn is coming up," she warns.

Ordinarily, this would get him going, as Caden doesn't like anyone telling him how to drive, but he knows she's just trying to help. So he does as she says and puts on his blinker.

"Thanks. I wouldn't want to miss another turn," he teases.

Jeri shrugs her shoulders. "No big deal. It's so quiet out here, no one would notice. The cows won't turn you in for doing an illegal turn in the middle of the road," she says with a smile.

They drive on in comfortable silence. Saul scratches the ears of Butch and Sundance as they lay on either side of him. "So have you been to every state, Saul?" Caden asks him after a while.

"Just about. The only one left is Hawaii. You can't drive to Hawaii," he jokes.

Caden's eyes widen at the realization that he's been to all forty-nine states. "No, you sure can't," he agrees.

"So what's the most interesting job you've ever done?" Jeri asks.

"Once I drove a truck full of chickens," he says. "That was kind of weird."

She wrinkles her nose. "Sounds kind of gross."

He chuckles. "Well, I felt bad for the chickens. That summer in Kansas got pretty hot, and they were really crammed in there." He clears his throat. "Sometimes they didn't make it."

"Ugh. That's awful," she laments.

"I know. If you ever have to unload a truck full of dead chickens, that's not something you forget," he continues.

"Oh, Uncle Saul. That's terrible."

"You don't have to tell me. I was there," he states.

"Oh, I know," Jeri gets all excited. "Where did you two get married? Was it on one of your romantic road trips?"

Saul looks his niece in the eye. "I thought you knew all of this."

She shakes her ponytail back and forth. "No, Uncle. I swear I don't."

He clears his throat. "Goldie and I were married down at the courthouse. Her parents weren't warming up to me as fast as I had hoped, but I wasn't going anywhere just the same. I mean, I wasn't going to stay away from their daughter just because they thought I should, so I did the sensible thing. I asked her to marry me, and she said yes."

His words stir up something in Caden, something he wants to ignore, but can't. "So how long were you together before you married?"

"I married Goldie seventy-five days after the day we met," he states.

Jeri whips around to stare down her uncle. "Are you serious?"

He shrugs his sagging shoulders and gives her a small smile. "What can I say? When you know, you know."

"But that's crazy. You can't know anyone that well after just seventy-five days. That's like two and a half months, Uncle Saul."

He chuckles again. "I knew after a month." He slaps his knee. "Heck, I knew after talking to her for five minutes that I could listen to her talk for the rest of my life." He pauses for half a second. "Fortunately for me, God smiled on me, and I was blessed to have her in my life for longer than I'm sure I deserved."

Jeri feels foolish when her eyes water. She can't imagine anyone talking about her so forthright and honest, much less that sweet. "But how did you know after just two months? I mean, that's just crazy."

"Is it, Jeri? Think about what I'm saying. You've known people who were together for five years or more before they married, and now they're divorced. If you don't know someone after five years, do you think you'll ever really know them?" He hugs himself a little. "I don't think it's always about how well you know them. I think it's about the commitment you're both willing to make to each other. Love is not always about feeling safe and secure in what you know. It's about facing the unknown together. It's about being willing to be there for someone else. It's about putting their wants and needs in front of yours."

"Is that why you didn't have children?" Jeri asks in a much quieter tone. "Was it because one of you didn't want to be a parent?"

Saul is quiet for so long, Jeri thinks she should apologize, but she really wants to know.

"No," he finally says, and there is no mistaking the sadness in his voice. "We weren't able to have children."

Jeri blushes. "I'm so sorry. I had no idea. I just thought it was a choice you made."

"I know you didn't know. I've never said much about it because it was too painful for Goldie to talk about. She could barely say it aloud," he explains. "There's more than one reason you're so special to me," he teases, but she hears the sorrow in his words. "You're the daughter I never had," he adds.

"Turn right up there," Jeri says to Caden as she stares into her phone. She's afraid if she looks at her uncle she's going to burst into tears. His heartfelt words are so sweet. She feels bad that she's jealous of the love he knew with Goldie. She doesn't think she'll come close to knowing what it feels like to have someone love her that much because she doesn't deserve it. Jeri's never been brave. She's not a risk taker. If someone told her they loved her after a few months, she'd call them crazy.

thirteen

Caden pulls up to the submarine museum. He meets Saul's eye in the rearview mirror. It's like an unspoken agreement passes between them because Saul opens the car door. "Give me a few minutes with just the dogs, would ya ? I need some air. You two were too loud for too long," he growls before he steps out of the car. Butch and Sundance follow close behind. Saul slams the door just enough to make Jeri jump in the passenger seat.

Caden turns to look at Jeri. "What do you think of your uncle's words?" he asks in earnest.

"What do you mean?" she asks cautiously.

"About decidin' to commit to each other," he supplies before he takes hold of her hand. "I know we haven't known each other long, but there's somethin' there. I feel it. I think we owe it to ourselves to consider the possibilities."

"The possibilities of what, Ca-den?" she says as she stares him down. "I listened to what my uncle said too. I didn't hear anything in there about possibilities. I heard him say he knew. Period."

Caden exhales slowly, or at least he tries to. His impatience gets in the way. "I know how I feel about you. I think I've made that very clear. I'm there. It's you who has the problem," he says about the time he regrets using that particular choice of words.

"That's hardly a proposal," Jeri grumps.

"Is that what you want?" he demands.

"If I have to ask for a proposal, how much can it really mean?" Jeri all but yells as her eyes water all over again. She starts to open her door, but Caden leans across and pulls it shut.

"Stop runnin' away," he whispers, and it tears her in two just a little. But she's not ready for whatever comes next.

Her eyes widen as she stares at his hand attached to her door. "Who says I'm running from you?" she replies in a small voice that sounds like she's in a dark closet all by herself.

He didn't think her tin-can car could get any smaller, but it feels like he's being crunched on all sides when he sees the look of fear in Jeri's face. He hates that he may have put it there. He releases the door handle, making sure he gives her her space as he inches away slowly. They stare out the front window awkwardly at Saul who shuffles around following Butch Cassidy and Sundance Kid around on the small patch of grass running alongside the museum parking lot.

"Guess I'll go in the museum with Saul," he offers.

"That would be nice," she says in a stiff tone.

Caden crawls out of the car like a scolded schoolboy. He can't believe how fast things went south. He's never had this much trouble with any other woman. Jeri is so hard to read. She's hot and cold. She acts interested, but then she backs off whenever he tries to make a move. She says it's because they have to maintain a professional relationship, but he's not so sure.

He thinks she uses her work as a shield because she's afraid of falling for him. Caden rewinds their latest conversation. He can't believe he came close to proposing. What was he thinking? They haven't even been on a date yet. It must have been Saul's inspiring story, but it was more than that. Because he was right there with him. It's not just transference.

Caden knows how he feels, and it hits him right in the gut. He'd rather be alone on a Friday or Saturday night or any other for that matter, which he has been a lot lately, thanks to baby-faced Bairn and his tattletale mouth, the Judge, and Julie, his soon-to-be P. O. officer, by the way that letter read. He's going to be spending many dry nights at home, not drinking a cold beer, and not watching sports on his favorite stool. He won't be doing much of anything he enjoys. His schedule has officially been interrupted. All the things he looks forward to at the end of the week are on hold.

But none of that comes close to bothering him like the idea that Jeri, the girl who has quickly embedded herself in his every thought, action, and motivation, is giving him the serious brush off. If she's doing it to drive him crazy on every level, it's working.

Caden glances in her direction as she squats beside her dogs. Her ponytail keeps falling over the side of her adorable neck, and she keeps flipping it back as if it's nothing more than an annoyance and not what he's been smelling for the last two hours in the car. Coconut, strawberry, and he can't name what other ingredients. All he knows is his olfactory is in overdrive. He turns away from the object of his affliction and kicks a rock across the parking lot. He's never been so love struck. Not even in high school when the sight of a squad of cheerleaders coming around the corner straight at him left him momentarily starstruck for like half a second, and he had to remind himself to breathe before he took the wrong step and ended up on his face.

"Caden," Saul calls out.

"Yep," he answers.

"Are you ready to go?"

He ducks his head, refusing to look at Jeri again. "Yep," he replies as he takes a few steps forward. Saul and Caden walk the plank that leads to the beached submarine's doorway. The two men duck as they step inside. Minutes later, the door closes. Caden didn't think he was claustrophobic, but now he's not so sure as they line up single file in the narrow hallway. He's used to working in the deep, dark confines of a salt mine, but that darkness has a vastness to it. This is all lit up, enabling him to see how much space he doesn't have.

"Welcome aboard, everyone," the young blonde-haired guy dressed in dull Navy blues, crisp button-up shirt and matching pants held up by a plain belt, booms out from the front of the line. "My name is Zack. I will be your host for the duration of this virtual submersion into what I call subworld," he says with a playful wink. There are a few collective groans in the audience, but Saul and Caden share a chuckle or two.

"I like this guy," Saul says in his deep, gravelly voice that echoes off the walls.

"Thank you," Zack replies. "Monetary tips are appreciated but not required," he rattles off as he starts walking backward. "What you see here are the sleeping quarters. They are a bit cramped, but they serve their purpose. We will be walking through the kitchen shortly, or in Navy terms, the galley. Today's Navy men eat a little better than they did back then, I suspect. They emphasize a healthy diet full of Vitamin C. Lots of fresh vegetables and fruit. They also eat a lot of soups. The average submarine carries up to 160 pounds of food for each man or woman on board."

Saul and Caden wander around the kitchen slowly, peering over and around the others in the tour. Caden is more fascinated than he thought he would be. "How does a submarine know where other ships are, so they don't run into them?" a lady asks.

"That's an excellent question. When a submarine surfaces, it has the ability to search out vessels it cannot see by using a system called a radar boom. This system picks up vessels that are farther away and out of sight," he replies.

Caden thinks he needs a radar boom system to detect Jeri's shutdown modes so he can prevent them from happening. He can't fight his grin at the thought, and then he does a mental check as he tries to shove her out of his head once more and focus on Zack's informative, yet entertaining tour.

"Next, we're going to the mess area. This is where the crew meets to discuss strategies and such."

"Is it true submarines are run off nuclear energy?" the same lady asks, and Caden thinks she's certainly done her homework.

"Yes, but they also use electricity."

"Is the use of nuclear energy a bit concerning?" she prods, and Caden wonders what she's getting at.

Zack's smile falters a little, but he keeps it in place. "Every submarine crew is well prepared for emergencies. That is a big part of their job as well. They do routine drills called *damage control drills* for that specific purpose. The United States Navy takes the safety of their crew and country seriously, ma'am. They wouldn't use nuclear energy to run a submarine if it wasn't tested and proven many times over," he says with a curt tone that states *no more questions* as he follows with a charming smile before stepping off to the side. "Speaking of potential dangers, this brings me to the next part of the tour. Occasionally, a submarine could experience a fire. For this reason, the entire crew must know how to don protective gear and attach the appropriate connecting hoses inside the submarine in absolute darkness," he pauses for effect, "as we just discussed, safety is key on a submarine."

Saul raises his hand.

"Yes, sir," Zack says as he points at him.

"Does a submarine have to come close to shore to get supplies?"

Zack's bright blues eyes light up. "That's an excellent question as well. I haven't had anyone ask me that in a long time."

Saul nudges Caden. "I think I'm his favorite," he jokes in a voice that is not near as quiet as he thinks it is.

Zack laughs a little at Saul's observations before continuing with his answer. "The most common way for a submarine to get supplies is from a helicopter. A box is lowered slowly down on a wire. The helicopter notifies the crew once the box is atop the sub. Trained crew members then exit the sub while it's surfaced. They crawl up on top and get the box to transport the supplies inside the sub."

"They crawl out of the sub while it's in the water?" a kid says in an awe-filled voice. "That's so cool."

Zack claps his hands once and points at the kid. "Yes, it is. Why don't you c'mon up here. You can be my volunteer for the next part of the tour."

The dark-haired boy weaves his way through the small

crowd, bumping a few elbows as he goes. Caden feels his excitement as he rushes by him. "What do I get to do?" the kid asks as he looks up at Zack.

"Before I give you an order, I need to know your name," Zack says in a solemn voice.

"My name is Hudson. You can call me Hud," he answers in a pre-teen voice that takes Caden back to simpler days when the love of his life was a blue-eyed, brown-haired German shorthair named Magpie. She was a wonderful traveler and the best playmate.

Zack gives him a hardy handshake. "Nice to meet you, Hud. As for what we're going to do, I don't know yet. Let's see what comes up, shall we?" He leans down and looks the kid in the eye. "The most important rule on a submarine is to always be prepared."

Hudson nods his head. "Okay."

The group follows along behind the tall blonde-haired Zack and the shorter, stockier, Hudson. They walk down some steps. Saul trips a little, but he rights himself. Caden grabs him by the arm. "Are you alright?"

"Yeah. Just this hip of mine. It likes to do its own thing once in a while. That's all," Saul growls because he doesn't like the extra attention.

Zack cups his hands to his mouth. "This is where the torpedoes were stored. Does anybody know what they are used for?"

"To attack," a man speaks up from behind Caden's ear, and he instinctively moves a little closer to Saul.

"Not exactly," Zack answers. "Anyone else want to guess?"

"For defense," Caden replies.

"That's right," Zack says before turning to Hudson.

"Now. If we were to release a real torpedo, it might go something like this. You would say 'In the window tube five and tube eight' and then I would push the release buttons. Are you ready to call it out?"

Hudson nods his head again. Zack nudges him. "Okay, call it out."

Hudson startles. "Oh, okay. Um, in the window tube five and tube eight," he says in an unenthusiastic tone.

Zack looks disappointed. He turns with wide eyes to face Hudson. His hands are on his hips. "Hud. We are out at sea. We are going in stealth, so the enemy can't see us as we track their location. We've just been fired on. Our response time is crucial. You gotta yell it so everyone knows we are under attack." He stares him down. "Can you let us know we are under attack?"

Hudson cups his hands to his mouth, throws his head back, and yells, "In the window! Tube five and tube eight!"

Zack claps him on the shoulder. "That's more like it. Excellent work. Excellent." He looks out at the crowd with a look of satisfaction. "Everyone give Hud here a round of applause for his surprising show of force." They all laugh a little as they clap their hands. Hudson stands beside Zack with a grin on his face. He takes a few bows. The noise dies down, and Zack shakes his hand one more time. "Give the Navy a call in about six years if you want to serve your country."

The rest of the tour is a bit dull compared to the torpedo room, but Caden enjoys every bit of it. Between the light in Saul's eyes and the entertaining comments of Zack, Caden is happy he came along, despite Jeri being unimpressed with his attempts at getting to know her on a more personal level.

The door opens, and they walk toward the light. Caden

digs through his wallet and pulls out a twenty-dollar bill that he drops in the donation tub that Hudson hugs to his middle while he posts up at the outside door. Saul leans in toward Hudson. "Way to go, sport. You gotta good set of lungs on ya."

Jeri traces the edge of the parking lot at a brisk walk.

"You been walkin' since we went in?" Saul hollers at her.

She doesn't answer as she starts toward them. Butch and Sundance trail her on their short little legs. Their tongues hang out as they click-click across the cement. Jeri makes a show of looking at her watch. "Yes. I was getting my steps in," she answers Saul while not looking at Caden. "Was it a good tour?"

"Yeah. It was terrific," Saul replies. "Truly."

"Well, good. I'm glad." She gets out her phone.

"What're you doin'?" Caden asks her since she seems determined to ignore him.

"Lookin' for a place to eat," she says while staring at her phone.

"I brought food," he says.

She looks up at him with exasperation in her expression. "I meant real food. Not snacks from a gas station," she snarks.

"I have real food. I even brought a cooler," he says. "With drinks, and plates, and everythin'," he pops off.

"Fine," she says as she returns to her phone.

"Now what are you doin'?" he demands. He can't believe she didn't even say thank you.

"Looking for a park," she says.

"We could eat here," Saul offers. "In this parking lot."

"I am not eating in a submarine museum parking lot," she spits out. Caden has no idea what has her so fired up.

"Okay," he says. "Just tell me where to go, and I'll go there."

Her hand flies to her hip. "Don't get all cutesy and submissive with me, Caden. You know what you did," she says as she points a finger at his face.

Saul turns on his heel and starts walking towards the car.

Caden is so confused. "Yeah. I went inside a submarine on a tour with *your* uncle because you're too scared to go in there," he shout-whispers.

"To score brownie points with me," she shout-whispers back. "It hardly counts."

"What bee is in your bonnet? I mean what happened between the time I went in there and the time I came out," he asks in an impatient voice. "Because *something* did."

"Need I remind you that you gave me the worst proposal in *history* before you up and left me with my two dogs for an hour and seven minutes," she continues. "And then while you're in there wandering around having fun, I'm out here walking the dogs in the hot sun. There's no food. There's no water. They could have overheated, and I don't even have any aspirin to revive them," she says as her lower lip trembles.

"But that's not the half of it. The Judge, your dad's friend, e-mailed me and told me I am not to act on Julie's behalf as a P. O. officer." She openly glares up at him. "I've never been told specifically not to do something, as if I'm not capable of getting the job done. I know enough to be a P.O. officer, especially for you. All I have to do is follow you around everywhere you go to be sure you don't get yourself thrown in jail again by just being who you are," she says with a flourish as she waves her hands around wildly like she's some sort of flightless bird trying to take off.

"I asked him to not have you as a P. O. officer because I'm tryin' to date you," Caden grounds out.

Jeri feels terrible and ecstatic at the same time, neither of which she wants Caden to know. "Well, I didn't know that. I had no idea. You told the Judge you want to *date me?*" she squeaks. "He obviously thought I would," she muses. "How *embarrassing.*"

"No, I did not tell him that in those words. I told him I was personally invested in our relationship and to work with you in a professional capacity would create a potential conflict of interest for me."

She continues her stare-down. "So you basically told him you want to date me," she declares again. "Just because you said it in a more knowledgeable way doesn't change anything about the content," she accuses, but he hears a softness in her voice.

"So are you ready to sign a love contract with me?" he teases, but he can't seem to keep the hope out of his tone.

"Um, no. Not even," she wrinkles her nose.

"Thanks for lettin' me down easy."

She is flattered by his persistence. There's no denying her attraction to him, but she is tired of his not accepting what she feels to be a perfectly rational explanation as to why it is terrible timing for them to start any sort of personal relationship. "You do realize you are in the grown-up world, right?" she barks. "We're not all floating around like fragile pieces of glass that require bubble wrap," she snaps.

Caden makes an incredulous face at her before snapping his fingers in her face. "Sit," he commands.

"Excuse me?" she replies with surprise in her tone.

He gives her a direct look. "You heard me. I told you to

sit," he commands again in the same authoritative voice he used the first time. She can't believe how hot it is.

"Um, why?"

"You're actin' like a vicious dog tryin' to bite my head off, so I was respondin' in kind," he says before he pivots and walks away. "I'm just gonna go stand over there where the more civilized people are," he calls out as he points toward Saul. Jeri stands in the place he left her, rooted to the spot. She's not taking one step toward Caden, not after he's been so awful to her.

"Come over if you get hungry. I might give you some leftovers," he taunts as he takes a big bite of sandwich minutes later. Her stomach growls, but her pride gets the better of her. It'll be a cold day in Hades before she accepts anything from that Neanderthal who talks with his mouthful as he leans against her car as if he owns it just like he owns her emotions.

fourteen

Jeri can't believe it's been two weeks since the whole parking lot debacle with Caden all but calling her a dog. She'd never been so insulted in her life. And she's been cheated on, a fact she's dying to tell Charmaine, save for the fact that it's so humiliating. But after suffering the silent treatment for two weeks, the longest she's ever carried on in a professional-capacity-only with Charmaine, her co-worker and best friend who treats her with the aloofness of two strangers passing on the street, she's more than ready to cave.

Jeri glances at the clock. It's three in the afternoon. There's only two hours left of her workday, but she can't go another second. Judging by the freeze-out Charmaine's been giving her, she's happy to stay a Dreamsicle forever.

"Fine. I'll tell you," Jeri announces.

Charmaine rolls her big brown eyes beneath her bright-green magnetic lashes and puckers her purple lips. She puffs out her chest covered by a plain knit top and shoves her sweater sleeves up to her elbows.

Jeri peeks below the desk and spies Charmaine's skirt that hovers a few inches above the floor. It's so out of character. Jeri leans back in her chair. "Are you..." She stops a second and studies her co-worker more closely. "Are you imitating me?"

Charmaine raises one eyebrow in warning. "Maybe."

Jeri stares at the bun atop her friend's head. "You never wear a bun."

Charmaine gives a shiver. "I know. I've been itchy all day. This outfit makes me feel so old," she drags out the last word.

Jeri slaps her desk. "I should be offended, you know. I know you don't like my clothes, but I didn't think you'd go so far as to dress like me just to make fun," she warns.

Charmaine throws her hands up in the air. "How else was I gonna get you to talk to me? You've been like a steel trap over there. I know somethin's goin' on between you and that miner, so why don't you just tell me?"

Jeri can't believe how much her words tear her up. "Nothing is going on between us."

"So that's the problem," Charmaine says. She nods her head excitedly. "Hmm mmmm. You *want* there somethin' to be goin' on though." She giggles. "Ooh, girl. You've got it bad. I can't believe I didn't figure this out sooner. He's got you on the hook, and you're too proud to tell 'em."

Jeri wiggles in her seat. "I'm not going to pretend I even know what that means, only to say that I assure you *no man* has me on a hook, a string, or anything else. I am my own woman. I don't need a man to make me feel special," she states before giving Charmaine the stink eye. "You're the one who told me I don't need a man to define me, so what are you saying?"

Charmaine shakes her head back and forth. "No, girl.

What I said was you don't need a liar and a cheat defining who you are. A good man, especially one that looks like Wolverine, is a whole 'nother thing. That man is as fine as the good Lord ever made one, and you'd be a fool to let him go."

Jeri frowns at her friend. "I can't believe you'd say that sort of thing to me." She exhales slowly. "I haven't even told you about his lame proposal."

Charmaine's eyes about bug out of her head. "The man proposed? And you didn't tell me until now? And you said no?" she exclaims.

"He also called me a dog if that makes the fact I told him *no* any better," Jeri muses.

"He did not," Charmaine challenges in a voice that says she kind of believes that he did.

"He commanded me to sit in the middle of a parking lot," Jeri argues. "Twice. And then he told me if I couldn't stop biting his head off, he was going to go somewhere more civilized," Jeri adds, but Charmaine's laughing too hard to hear the rest of it.

"I can't believe that boy told you to sit in the middle of a parking lot." She gets herself together, sort of. "I'm trying to picture this. What parking lot?"

Jeri shrugs her shoulders. She'd rather not say, especially since Charmaine is being so insensitive and not taking her side. "The parking lot outside the submarine museum he went into with my Uncle Saul," she explains, knowing what's probably coming next.

"He went to a museum with your Uncle Saul, and you two aren't even dating," she says in a voice that she's in disbelief.

"*I know,* alright" Jeri admits. "The guy showed up at my

house at sunrise with no warning. He was all excited to go on some road trip. He even packed a cooler with food for a picnic," she adds. "I guess it was kind of sweet."

"Dang right, it was sweet. I'd be happy if a guy I dated could make himself a dam sandwich. It's two pieces of bread and a slice of ham in the middle. How hard is that?" Charmaine asks.

Jeri can't help but giggle at Charmaine's comment. "I don't know," she eyes her friend. "Did I make a mistake?"

Charmaine tilts her head to the side. "How long have you known the guy?" she asks.

"Like twenty-four days if you don't count the night Miles walked in here with that thousand-dollar check. Otherwise, it's twenty-five," Jeri answers before Charmaine can take another breath.

"So you've been keepin' track," Charmaine notes.

"Um, yeah. The guy proposed. I was trying to decide how crazy it is that it kind of feels right," Jeri says as she stares at the floor.

"I don't think you're crazy," Charmaine says in a quiet voice.

Jeri's head pops up. "You don't?"

"No crazier than people who go to hook up with complete strangers or people who have one-night stands," Charmaine says.

"Gee, that's reassuring," Jeri replies in a sarcastic voice.

"Does the guy seem like a man who hands out marriage proposals like candy?" Charmaine asks.

Jeri considers her question. "No."

"Has he ever asked anyone else to marry him?" she continues.

Jeri doesn't know how she knows, but she does. "No."

"Are you like a mega-rich sugar momma and you're not tellin' me?" Charmaine questions.

Jeri is so confused. "No?"

"Is there any other reason this man would want to marry you other than love?" Charmaine asks, and Jeri finally gets it.

A smile spreads across her face. "No," she says with certainty.

Charmaine points a knowing finger at her friend. "There's your answer. He's not crazy, and neither are you." She gives Jeri a wink. "Remember this conversation when you're choosing your maid-of-honor."

"Yep," Jeri answers, but her mind is somewhere else. She can't be in love after twenty-five days, can she?

———

It's been a month since their trip to the submarine museum. Jeri has been radio silent. Caden can't believe how childish she's being. He's been by Saul's once a week. They've played cards. Her name hasn't come up once. Caden doesn't know how much more he can take. He knows Jeri's the woman for him, just like he knows he's the guy for her. He's trying to trust Saul's advice, to give her space so she knows what she's missing. But it's hard.

Caden rolls his bike behind a van. He sits on it, waiting for the yellow car to leave. He decides if she's not gone in the next ten or fifteen minutes, he's leaving. Caden's patience is rewarded when he sees her yellow car pull out onto the road. He wastes no time as he strides across the parking lot and slips in the apartment building when someone walks out. Caden heads for Saul's apartment and knocks on the door before turning the knob and walking in.

"Saul," he calls out, but doesn't get an answer. "Maybe he's in the bathroom," he ponders, and then feels bad for walking right in. He sits down at the kitchen table to wait a second or two, but then he hears a groaning sound. Panic fills him, and he heads toward the sound. Caden nudges the bathroom door and is shocked to find Saul lying on his bathroom floor, mostly covered with a towel.

"I think I broke something," Saul groans as he clutches his towel. "I was climbing into the shower, and I slipped and fell."

Caden cringes at the grimace in the old man's face. It's clear he's in a lot of pain. "What can I do?"

Saul looks him in the eye. "Can you wrap me up and carry me out of here? I need to go to the hospital, but I can't afford an ambulance."

Caden thinks of his motorcycle. "Do you have a car? I only have my motorcycle."

Saul groans again. "Get my phone off my bed, and call Jeri," he orders.

Caden runs for the bedroom. He grabs up the phone and scrolls through the contacts. Jeri picks up on the third ring.

"Uncle Saul?" she asks.

Caden clears his throat. "It's, um, Caden. Your uncle fell. He needs a ride to the hospital, and I only have my motorcycle."

"Are you seriously making up medical excuses now to see me?" she accuses.

He can't believe how ridiculous she's being. "No. Your uncle is hurt. Are you going to get your butt over here, or do I call someone else I know who has a car?" he demands.

"Why are you at his apartment?" she asks as she starts looking for a place to turn around on the road.

"Jeri. This is no time to argue. Please hurry. It's an emergency, but he doesn't want me to call the ambulance. He thinks his hip is broken," he explains.

"You better not be messing with me. I'm turning around. I'm on the road." She pauses. "Can you sit with him until I get there?"

"Of course," he answers.

"Grab my wallet off my dresser," Saul calls. "It has my insurance information in it."

Caden does as he asks. He slips the phone and wallet into his jacket pocket. "Where's your phone charger?"

"It's in my bedroom. Plugged into the wall," Saul replies.

Caden snags it. "Got it."

It's just a few minutes, but it feels like forever as Caden sits on the bathroom floor by Saul wishing he could do something, anything, to make him feel more comfortable, but he knows he can't. So he waits impatiently until he hears the apartment door open. "We're in the bathroom," he yells right before Jeri pops her head in.

"Oh, Uncle Saul," she declares as tears roll down her cheeks.

"I'm sorry, girl. I'm in my birthday suit," her uncle says in apology.

Jeri turns around to give her uncle privacy. "What do I need to do?"

Caden stands up. "Stay out of my way. I'm going to carry your uncle out to your car," he says in a gruff voice.

"What?" Jeri demands. "That's a terrible idea."

"It's my idea, and this is my apartment," Saul groans.

"Fine, but it could do more damage if you're not moved correctly," Jeri scolds.

"There's nothing he can do that a doctor can't fix," Saul argues.

"I'll get the car ready," Jeri concedes as Saul's dangling foot hits her in the back. Caden has already scooped him up.

"We're right behind ya," he gets out.

Jeri holds the apartment door open before closing it behind them. She turns the doorknob once to be sure it's locked then follows Caden who cradles her uncle. Saul has always been bigger than life to her, but now he's a frail elderly man clinging to Caden's broad back as he strides down the hall with ease, as if her uncle weighs ten pounds. Jeri slips around them to open the outside door. Somehow, Caden manages to crawl into the backseat with Saul on his lap. They scoot to the middle so she can get the door closed.

Jeri pulls in under the ER awning. She rushes inside to find staff to roll out a stretcher. They arrive at the car in seconds. Caden emerges from her car like a giant climbing out of a clown car as he stands to his full height. An EMS worker gives them a funny look when they discover Saul is naked beneath the towel.

"He fell getting into the bathtub," Jeri offers.

"Are you his next of kin?" EMS asks.

Saul grabs a hold of her hand. "She's my niece, but she may as well be my daughter." He points at Caden. "He's my friend. He has my billing information."

The EMS worker glances at the pulse oximeter that reads his oxygen and pulse rate. "What's your pain on a scale of one to ten?"

Saul catches his breath. "I'd say about a six or seven," he answers between his gasping and grimacing.

Jeri grabs a hold of the EMS guy's arm. "That's a nine or ten in most people's book," she warns.

The EMS worker nods. "Got it. By the looks of his pulse, I'd say he's in considerable pain."

Caden white knuckles the side of the stretcher. "It's going to be fine, Saul. You're in good hands now. We'll just be out here waiting," he assures him.

Jeri releases her uncle's hand and holds out a flat palm to Caden. "Give me his wallet. I can take it from here."

Caden slaps the wallet in her hand. "I'm not going anywhere, Jeri. I'm staying here until your uncle comes out of surgery."

"Why? You don't need to do that. I'm here for Saul. He'll be fine," she says in a trembling voice.

He lays a hand on her arm. "But who will be here for you?"

Jeri opens her mouth again to argue but closes it. It's been so long since someone was there for her when she most needed them. She's not sure how she feels about it being Caden, but hospitals really aren't Charmaine's thing. She walks up to the man sitting on the other side of the glass. She slides Saul's insurance information in the drop slot. He scans it in his machine and gives it back. She drops her business card in the slot. His eyebrows raise when he sees her card.

"I'm Saul's niece. That's my cell phone number. Please call me if you need anything," she says. "I might go wait outside," she adds as she looks around at all the people hovering, waiting to be seen. She doesn't like to think about all the potential germs floating around in the room.

"Want to go wait in the car?" she asks Caden.

He eyes the lobby that is three-fourths of the way full. "Sure," he says, thinking her car is a little smaller than he'd prefer, but at least it's quiet. They walk across the lot in silence.

She gets in the front seat. She's confused when he crawls in the back. "What are you doing?" she asks as she turns to see him doing his best to curl his six-foot two linebacker-like body onto the tiny backseat of her car. She gets out and opens the trunk. She grabs up her two favorite fuzzy blankets and a pillow before closing it. She walks around the front of her car and climbs back in before tossing him the pillow and a blanket. "Might be a little more comfortable."

He accepts them. "Thanks."

"It's the least I can do. Thanks for rescuing Uncle Saul," she says. "You saved me from a night of Bingo down at the senior center," she adds.

Caden grins at the thought. "Do your criminals hide out down there or something?" he teases.

"No. Once a month I take Uncle Saul to Bingo night. He so seldom wants to get out for anything, so when he does, I can't say no," she explains. "He doesn't even grocery shop anymore. He has his food delivered to his door with that new service since the virus came out."

"It is handy, you gotta admit. And, he's helping out a college kid," Caden points out.

"Yeah, I suppose. There are some good things that came out of this horrible virus trying to shut down all social interaction on any level," Jeri grumps.

"Bingo night, huh," Caden muses. "You're a good niece."

Jeri shrugs her shoulders. "I enjoy spending time with Saul." She exhales slowly. "He never complains about my cooking, which could be called marginal," she admits. "Cooking is so tiresome. You have to pay attention to the recipe so you don't leave any ingredients out. Then you have to pay attention so you don't burn it. Then you have to do all the clean up after."

"So you don't cook?" Caden asks with a small amount of dread. He can't imagine being with someone who doesn't cook.

"I cook. I just don't like it," she adds. She raises a finger. "But, should I ever marry, I'm not washing dishes *and* cooking. I'll do one or the other. Women work too, so we shouldn't have to do all the domestic work alone."

Caden snorts. "Is that all you're worried about for marriage?"

Jeri turns to look at him. "What do you mean?"

He looks right back. "What do you mean, what do I mean? A girl like you surely has a list for her future groom, and I'm sure it has more than two items on it."

Jeri feels strange inside. "You want to know my potential groom list?"

Caden sticks out his tongue at her, and it reminds her of a junior-high boy, so why does she find it charming? "Why not? I mean, I proposed once already, and you said no. So how much more awkward could it get between us?" he asks, but his voice is so quiet she barely hears the last four or five words.

"Fine. I'll tell you, but you've got to tell me yours," she insists.

He props his chin on his hand. "What makes you think I have a list?"

Jeri feels caught. "I just figured a guy like you has one," she says in the most unattached, unassuming voice as possible.

"A guy like me?" Caden prompts.

Jeri's hand heads for her hair. She's a hair twirler, especially when she's nervous. She stops before she gets there and fiddles with her earlobe. "All I mean is I'm sure a guy like you doesn't have trouble getting any numbers when you're out at the bars?"

Caden bristles at her words, even though they're absolutely true. "What makes you think I'm out at the bars picking up girls?"

"You ended up in jail because you got into a fight at the bar," she blurts out.

"Yeah. I was there drinking a beer and watching a game. There's no crime in that," he argues.

"You telling me girls don't try to talk to you when you're sitting at the bar with your beer looking...all like..." she pauses and exhales slowly, "how you look," she finishes.

"A guy can say *no* just like a girl," Caden offers.

She snorts. "No guy I ever knew," she answers in a voice filled with disgust.

"Maybe I'm not every guy," he states as his eyes search hers for any acknowledgment that she accepts his truth.

She lifts her chin. "Well maybe I'm not every girl," she throws right back.

"Well, okay then," Caden says with a smile on his face because whether she realizes it or not, she walked right into the trap he didn't know he was laying.

"Okay," Jeri agrees, and then she turns back around. She doesn't know what just happened, other than her admitting she's the same type of person as Caden. That's not what she was trying to do at all. Why does every conversation they have end with her feeling like she fell into a hole he dug for her to step into? Even though she knows it, she's not sure she wants to climb out of it. Caden is so...so Caden. She muses as she tries in vain to ignore his presence filling up the backseat of her car.

"You'll wake me if I fall asleep, right?" he asks.

"Of course," she says as she leans her seat back just a little and leans up against a corner of the blanket that lies between her and the side of her door and window.

Hours later, it's Caden who hears Jeri's phone going off on the passenger seat while she snores into the door, causing a small foggy shape on the glass. He lays a hand on her shoulder and goes to shake her but decides to rattle her instead as he leans close enough to breathe his warm breath on the back of her neck as his lips almost touch her earlobe.

"Jeri" he whispers. Her hand flies up in response to swat at him. "Jeri," he speaks her name a little louder and nips her earlobe, about the time she's wide-awake.

The back of her hand swipes at her mouth before her fingertips and palm graze the side of his face. Her lips chase his. They don't stop until they find what they're after. Her warm breath mingles with his. Caden curses the seat between them as his hand releases its grip on the side of her seat and flies to the back of her perfect neck. His thumb digs into her nape just slightly as he increases the pressure of his lips on hers, and she sinks into him for one delicious second.

He falls against her as he tries to get closer. Their teeth bump against each other, and it's jarring.

Jeri jerks out of his gentle grasp. "We need to go and get Saul. We need to go check on Saul."

For the first time in his life, Caden is without a response. "Yeah," he says, because he has nothing else to say. He felt that kiss in every part of his being, and that's never happened before. He's never come close to feeling the amount of heat Jeri's lips hold, and he's kissed more lips than he'd like to admit. It's almost as if she branded him, but in a good way.

He climbs out of her car in a stupor. It's as if he's been

struck by lightning. He knows he'll never feel this way about another woman. Ever. Jeri walks across the parking lot like nothing happened. Surely she felt the significance of a small earthquake going off beneath their feet, like the lowest measurement on the Richter scale.

"Are you coming?" she demands from where she stands at the door to the hospital.

Caden glances at his watch. "It's almost midnight?"

"No wonder I'm tired," Jeri muses.

They walk in together. "Jeri White?" a woman asks from the double doors across the room.

"That's me," Jeri answers before walking closer to Caden. She slips an arm through his. "Can he come back too?" Jeri asks in a warmer voice than Caden's ever heard coming from her lips when she's anywhere near him.

"Sure," the lady says.

They follow her down the hall and stop outside Room Seven. "He might be a little groggy because we have him on pain meds. They had to put him under to reset his leg. He fractured his left femur," the woman states.

Caden can't help but smile. "He pretty much called it."

Jeri swats at his chest with her hand. "Stop talking. I need to know what she's telling me," she adds by way of apology.

Ordinarily Caden would take offense at being scolded like a child, but he's stuck on the familiar way she talks to him and the feeling of the back of her hand on his chest. He scoots a little closer to Jeri and keeps eye contact with the nurse while he tries to focus on what she's saying and not on his proximity to Jeri. The words *overnight* and *home health aide* stick in his head as they walk into Saul's room. Caden can't help but notice Saul looks like he's been ran through a wringer.

Jeri rushes her uncle. She leans over and hugs him as lightly as she can. Tears roll down her cheeks. "Oh, Uncle Saul. I'm so sorry you broke your leg."

He pats her back gently. "It's okay, Jeri. I'm alright. It's going to be a while before I'm up and around, but that's alright. I'll figure it out," he says, and she can tell he's trying put on a brave front. Uncle Saul doesn't have that many friends, at least not ones who are in better shape than he is.

She supposes she could move in with him, but she can't work from home. There are times her work requires her to be gone for hours at a time, just like tomorrow. She panics inside.

"What is it, Jeri?" Saul asks as she pulls away from him. The worried look on his face is for her, and it makes her want to cry all over again. "Nothing, Uncle Saul. You just focus on getting plenty of rest so you can heal," she says as she squeezes his hand. "I need you."

Saul squeezes her back. "You silly girl. I'm not going anywhere."

The nurse pops back in and pointedly looks at the clock before looking at Jeri and then Caden. Jeri kisses her uncle on the forehead before standing up. "You're staying here overnight. So I'll be back tomorrow to see you."

"Sounds good," Saul answers.

Jeri and Caden walk out together. They're just outside when Caden turns to her. "This may not be my place, but I think I have the perfect solution for Saul staying home."

Jeri stops walking. "He can't afford a full-time CNA, not even a part-time one," she worries.

"That's good because my cousin isn't a nurse's aide.

She's just a college-age girl in between jobs, and she needs a place to live. She likes to take care of people, and she's really good at it," he assures her.

"And she would take care of a total stranger for no pay," Jeri says in a voice full of doubt.

"Um, no. She would take care of a total stranger for free food, rent, and Netflix access," Caden corrects her.

"Seriously?"

He throws his hands in the air. "Definitely. She's been living with her parents for about a week. They're going crazy, and so is she. They fight all the time. If she took care of your uncle, she could show her parents that she's more responsible than they think, and it would give her a little more freedom than she has right now while she's trying to figure out the next chapter in her life."

Jeri is so relieved she has the urge to hug him. "I'm so happy, I could kiss you," she gushes, and then she's instantly embarrassed as she remembers their kiss, but in all fairness, he snuck up on her in her sleep.

Caden smirks at her, but she sees something else in his eyes. Something that looks like promise. He reaches for her hand. "We could give it another go," he teases.

She turns slightly away from him while she digs for her keys to unlock her car. He goes around to the other side. They climb in in sync. She starts it up.

Caden clears his throat. "I was just teasing, Jeri. Don't get like that. Please."

She relaxes a hair. "I know," she says as she backs out.

He taps his fingertips nervously on his knees. "Good, because I wouldn't want to do anything to upset you," he says as he stares out the window. "At least not permanently," he adds.

They drive on in silence. Jeri pulls up next to his motorcycle outside her uncle's apartment. Caden reaches for his door but turns back to face her. "Jeri."

"Yeah," she says.

"For a minute I was just me and you were just you. It was the best moment I've had in a long time, if ever," he says as he lifts his head to meet her surprised gaze. Maybe it's the widening of her eyes, the new awareness between them, or the slight space between her lips as her bottom lip somehow becomes fuller before his very eyes that draws him in. He asks permission over and over the slower and closer he gets, and still, Jeri waits. It's as if she knows the amount of torture he's going through. Just when he thinks she's a statue made of stone, she tilts her head.

"I'm still in the moment," she whispers as her lips meet his in a kiss that's just as magical and hungry as the first one. His hands fumble with her hair piled atop her head. Jeri pulls away from him in confusion.

"I'm sorry," he says. "I just want to see your hair down. I want to feel it in my hands," he explains, feeling more and more like he's saying everything wrong as he searches her guarded expression.

A small smile forms on her lips as she reaches for her bun. Seconds later, her shoulder-length blonde hair tumbles down. She runs her hands through it, shaking her head while ducking her face, as if she's self-conscious.

Caden tips her chin back with his thumb. "Jeri. You're beautiful," he says as he dives in for another kiss.

Jeri knows she's falling hard and fast, but she shoves that thought from her mind as she clings to Caden, tilting her head a little to the side to get a better angle. The tiny space of her car that doesn't allow for anything between the two front seats becomes even smaller the longer their kiss goes on. Jeri feels like she's going to burn up where she sits. She pulls away first. "I've got a long day tomorrow. I've got to get home and get some rest," she whispers, knowing that sounds like a bucket of cold water.

Caden runs a thumb across her lip as light as a feather before skimming the side of her face with the back of his hand. "Alright," he says before he blasts through the barriers she tries to put up with a hard-and-fast kiss that tells her he's on the edge of reason.

Jeri feels thrilled at the thought that she put him there. He gives her his most charming smile. "Can't blame me for wantin' to stay in our midnight moment as long as possible," he says before giving her hand a squeeze. "I'll text you tomorrow about my cousin. I'm sure she'll do it, but I can't ask tonight. She's probably asleep."

fifteen

Jeri drives home on autopilot. She can't believe Caden has a cousin who is going to move into her uncle's apartment. She worries a little about the idea of a stranger sharing his one-bedroom apartment, but she doesn't have a better answer. She knows her uncle isn't ready to move out of his apartment into long-term care. She can't afford to pay for full-time care for him to stay home, and neither can he. He could move in with her parents who would probably take him, but she knows her uncle. He would never go for that.

Jeri thinks of what her life would be if she never met Caden, and she's shocked to realize how empty it would be. She's known him for such a short time. "Don't get all freaked out, Jeri. He's just a man," she scolds herself, but she knows she's lying to herself.

He's so much more than an ordinary guy. He's becoming someone she depends on, and this gives her a start. "He's a client. He's supposed to depend on me," she muses, but this isn't true either. The first thing that came up between them, he went over her head. He went straight to the top. The only good thing about all of it was the Judge didn't yell at her, which is strange. Judges in the city wouldn't put up with a client calling them directly. Jeri considers this.

"It's just because he lives in a small town, and everyone knows him there," she reasons. "It would be different if he lived in a city. He wouldn't be so special then," she grumbles, and then immediately feels bad.

"What is wrong with me?" she wonders as she pulls into her driveway. "When am I going to accept that some people are just genuinely nice? They do things for others because they want to. Period. They don't expect anything in return, and they don't cheat and lie like Miles and Brian did. Not every man is a liar. I just happen to find two bad ones," she says, opening her door and leaning over to pet Butch and Sundance, who whine and bark, scolding her for being gone for so long.

"I know, I know. I'm so sorry. Something came up. I had to take care of Uncle Saul," she explains as she follows them to the backyard. She watches them as they scurry around in the grass, doing their business. "Hurry up, guys. I'm tired. I'm ready to go to sleep. I've got a long week ahead of me. Tomorrow's only Wednesday."

She walks back inside and sits on a chair by the doggy door. Minutes later, it swings open as her dogs pile through it. She flips the three latches that hold it shut overnight. "Alright, guys. I'm going to bed," she mutters as she slips out of her clothes and into a long tee shirt. She climbs beneath the sheets and closes her eyes. "Aww, finally," she mutters.

Jeri wakes to the sound of the alarm clock. She pushes the button, resists the urge to throw it against the wall as she climbs out of bed and heads for the shower. She emerges twelve minutes later in a towel from a steamy bathroom. She's halfway down the hall when she realizes what she saw. She pauses mid-step and backtracks to peek around the hallway door to see Caden sitting on her couch as if he belongs there.

"Good morning," she growls.

He looks way too happy and awake for six-fifteen in the morning. "Hey. I heard back from my cousin," he says.

She gives him a thumbs up. "I'm just going to go get ready for work now," she says and runs off to her room. She can't believe her dogs didn't go ballistic at the sight of him. They usually yap twice as loud when anyone visits.

Minutes later, she heads for the kitchen. She doubles the coffee in the filter and switches the pot setting from half to full before starting it. She moves onto the skillet, cracking twice as many eggs. She lays a spliced bagel in her toaster oven. She throws four pieces of ham in the skillet next to the eggs. She leans over and grabs the cream cheese from the fridge, ignoring the good feelings she gets from the idea of sharing breakfast with someone else. Particularly Caden who has a way of putting her at ease even though she knows how hot his kisses make her and how sweet he can be with his words when he's completely honest. That's something she's never known before, a thought that almost makes her drop the table knife on the floor as she lays it on the countertop.

She removes the skillet from the heat as she turns to look at him once more. "Hope you like eggs over easy."

He eyes the stove and the toaster oven. "You put anythin' on a plate that I didn't make, darlin', and the only words you'll get from me is a thank you."

Jeri's heart flips over from the words he says, particularly *darlin'*, which is just ridiculous. Normally she would take offense at being called anyone's darlin'.

"Okay," she answers as she spreads a layer of cream cheese on each bagel before laying them on separate plates. She lines them with ham before gently placing the egg on top of that. She sprinkles a little pepper on each one before grabbing two forks. She lays them down on both sides of the island. She returns to the coffee pot to pour two cups.

"You take yours black?" she asks as she turns around to find him in her space. He lays the softest of kisses on her lips as she holds two cups of coffee. He pulls back. "I like mine with a little sugar," he teases as he reaches for his cup. She glances at the container behind her.

"The sugar's in there," she manages.

He gives her an ornery grin. "You're the sugar," he explains.

"Oh," she says as her heart trips just a little. She glances at the clock. "Shoot. I've got to hustle."

She's shocked to see half of his bagel is already gone as Caden leans over his plate holding his bagel in his hand, abandoning his fork. She picks up her bagel and leans over her plate. She loves egg yolk, but she hates the mess it makes. She takes a big bite and feels the egg run down her chin. She's mortified. Caden's eyes dance as he tosses a napkin at her. He covers his chin with his hand. "You've got somethin' just there," he teases, but it's light-hearted.

She wipes at her chin before taking another big bite. Caden's already done with his bagel. He sips at his coffee for a few seconds before setting it down on the countertop. He scribbles a name and a number.

"There's my cousin's name. There's her number. Give her a call when Saul's ready to go home. She'll pick him up," he says as he leans over and smooches her cheek. "Best bagel and coffee I've ever had," he says in all sexy-like in her ear before straightening back up and moseying toward her front door.

Jeri flushes clean to her toes. She feels so strange. She's not used to someone whispering warm fuzzies in her ear, as her Uncle Saul would say. At least that's what she thinks that just was because it certainly gave her the warm fuzzies, and tingles, and other feelings she has no words for. She's not used to a guy telling her he will do something, and then he actually does it. She wipes her face with her napkin once more.

She stares after Caden who stops in the middle of the room as if he feels her eyes on him. She doesn't know what to say that would begin to be adequate for everything he's done for her. She drops her guard, strides over to him, and throws her arms around him. "Thank you," she says as her voice catches. She stands on tiptoe to get closer to his ear.

He hugs her right back. "Of course. You know I'd do anything for you," he answers, and they both go still.

He lets go as suddenly as she grabbed a hold of him. His eyes are dark and uncertain as they search hers.

Jeri feels unsure of herself and where she stands with him, but there's one thing she is sure of—how well they fit together. She lays her hand on his chest and tilts her head back just a little as if she's asking for something. Caden doesn't disappoint as he leans down to meet her kiss, but this one is slow and unhurried. It whispers of promise if she would just be brave enough to step up and claim it.

Caden's phone vibrates in his pocket, waking him from whatever dream he walked into. He can't believe he showed up on her couch with no notice. Sure, Saul told him to right before he gave him his spare key to her place. At least that's what he tells himself because Saul did. That doesn't mean Caden had to do it. He couldn't believe how quickly Jeri adjusted to his being in her space.

She didn't yell at him or ask him what the heck he was doing on her couch at six-fifteen in the morning. She didn't even ask him where her dogs are, he realizes in the middle of his phone call, which he heard nothing of, as he stands in her house with his hand on her front door, unable to turn it.

"Your dogs are in the backyard," he tells her before opening her door and walking down her sidewalk.

———

"I'm sorry. Could you repeat everything you just said," he says to the other foreman.

The guy laughs. "What's her name?"

"Jeri," Caden gets out as he clears his throat. "Just tell me what you just said," he adds.

———

Jeri scarfs down most of her bagel while she tries to chew a bagel as fast as one can chew a chewy bagel without choking on it. She sips her coffee slowly to soften the bagel in her mouth as she rushes around the kitchen, tossing dishes in the sink. She cuts up the remainder of her bagel and divides it between Butch and Sundance's food bowls before squatting down to whistle through the dog door at the two dogs. They run through like it a couple of piggies on their way to the feeding trough, which arguably is an accurate description for the way they snort around as they gobble up their food.

Jeri fights the smile that's been on her face ever since Caden walked away after breakfast. She snatches up the paper with his cousin's information on it, stuffs it in her pocket, and glances at her watch. "Oh, snap. I gotta get going," she declares in a voice that is unusually bright for her this early in the day.

She's never been much of a morning person. Caden's voice whispers in her ear all the way to her car, throughout her drive, and up the stairs into the office where she runs smack into the back of Charmaine. "I'm so sorry," Jeri sings, minus the usual snark that accompanies anything she says before nine-thirty AM on a weekday.

Charmaine turns to face her friend. She's got her I-slept-hanging-halfway-off-my-couch-last-night-cause-I'm-still-wearing-the-cushion-pattern-on-my-face look going on. Jeri backs away slowly.

Charmaine stares at her friend in confusion through her alcohol-induced hangover. "What's goin' on with you, Miss Happy Pants?" she accuses as she plops down in her seat in her black yoga pants, black sweatshirt, and black ballet slippers—an ensemble that caused a great deal of discussion between the two of them nine months ago, the first time Charmaine wore it.

Jeri said it was nothing more than glorified sleepwear and Charmaine may as well put a sign on her chest that said *I stopped trying today*.

Charmaine said the yoga pants were the same as dress jeggings, and her ballet slippers were elegant because if famous New Yorkers could wear them on stage and inspire people to throw roses, she should be able to wear them to work to bail criminals out of jail.

Then Jeri accused her of wearing a sweatshirt from a superstore.

Charmaine said it wasn't a sweatshirt because it had jewels on the front.

Jeri said a kindergartener could have done a better job gluing those jewels on.

And then neither of them spoke to each other for the rest of the day.

"Nothing," Jeri says right before *best bagel and cup of coffee ever* bursts out of her like a song.

Charmaine's fingertips fly to her temples, which she starts massaging in circles. "Girl, you bout blast the hair right off my head with that tone-deaf pitch of yours. Don't ever do that again," she warns.

Jeri grabs up a red folder and notebook off her desk. She stuffs them in her messenger bag and hurries toward the door.

"Your shirt's on inside out and backwards," Charmaine comments like an afterthought.

Jeri stops in her tracks. "It is not. Is it?" she demands as she lays down her bag, sheds her sweater, and tugs at her knit shirt to try to see the inside tag before she notices the inside-out seams going down both sides. "Oh, shoot," she says before she shuts her office door, sinks down to her butt, and rips the shirt over her head to turn it right side in.

"Dang, girl. What're you doin'?" Charmaine's eyes about bug out of her head. Jeri's never been the type to undress in front of anyone, not even other females.

"I'm in a hurry," Jeri says as she tugs her shirt back over her head before she stands up, puts her sweater back on, and tosses her messenger bag over her shoulder. "Wish me luck. I've got a long morning in court. Thirteen appointments."

"Show me the money," Charmaine calls out at her retreating form before burying her face in her hands once more. "I gotta quit the bachelorette parties. This is just stupid," she grumbles as her Maroon 5 goes off beside her on the desk. "Don't Blame the Champagne, this is Charmaine," she grumbles.

sixteen

Jeri is irate. She can't believe Caden proposed to her in front of her Uncle Saul, who gives her the look he used to give her when he was threatening to paddle her if she didn't straighten up.

"You won't find a better man, Jeri." Uncle Saul warns her as if Caden isn't standing right in front of her.

Jeri frowns. "You can't force me to marry him," she argues, which is so stupid. Every part of her wants to say *yes*, so why is she hesitating? She points at his weak side. "If you hadn't broken your femur, I never would have kissed him, and we wouldn't be here. He wouldn't be asking me to marry him."

"You don't know that, Jeri," Caden protests. He can't believe he's still standing here, staring in the face of rejection. Again. Ever since he met Jeri, his pride has taken a beating, but he can't walk away. She's the one for him.

"I'd break my other leg if that's what it takes to get you to see what's good for you," Saul threatens.

Jeri's eyes narrow. "Did you two plan the first fall?" she accuses.

Caden's eyes widen. "Of course not. It was dumb luck that I found him when I did. I was goin' to go in, but I saw you were outside. So I waited because I didn't want you to think I was followin' you."

"So you *were* following me," Jeri accuses.

"No, I wasn't. I wanted to talk to your uncle," Caden insists.

"About me." Jeri gives him the evil eye.

"So what if he was following you, and so what if he wanted to talk to me about you," Saul bellows. "You're so stubborn you can't see a good, honest man when you meet one. What has this man done that is so terrible? He found me a caretaker. He sent you flowers. He's been nothing but good to you," he accuses. "He's nothing like the two lying cheaters you dated before him," he blurts.

Jeri's face flames. "Thanks, Saul, for reminding me of my mistakes."

"I'm not trying to make you feel bad, Jeri. I'm just saying I know Caden. He's a good guy. What problem do you have with a good guy?" he demands.

Jeri stomps her foot. "I can't do this right now. You guys are ganging up on me, and it's not fair." She stares Caden down. "No one is going to tell me how to live my life, especially not an egotistical, over-bearing know-it-all man, even if your kisses are wonderful. You remind me of Wolverine, and you have the biggest heart for people you love," she states.

Caden steps closer until he's looking down his nose at her. "I can't be somethin' I'm not, Jeri. I'm not sure what you're lookin' for, but you know where to find me if you change your mind," he says before he walks out of the apartment.

"You go after him," Saul bellows at his niece as he points at the door. "Right now."

Jeri sinks into the chair. "I can't."

"Why not?" Saul asks.

"Because I love him," Jeri answers.

"I don't understand."

"Neither do I," she says as the tears runs down her face.

They sit in silence for a while.

"I understand why you love him," Saul says but stops as if he's leaving the rest of the sentence open.

Jeri sits back in her chair. "You don't understand why he loves me."

Her uncle throws his hands up in the air. "If the shoe fits." He leans heavy on his cane as he stares at his niece whose face is downcast. "What are you afraid of?"

She looks up at him. "I'm afraid of losing myself if I get married."

Saul laughs out loud. "What the hell does that mean?"

Her hands fly out. "I'm glad my fear and anxiety is so amusing." She takes a deep breath. "You've met Caden. He's so big." She waves her hands. "Not just his physique. I'm talking about his personality. He's just so much."

"But he's a nice guy," Saul argues.

"Well, yeah," she agrees.

"Then what's the problem?"

"I'm afraid I'll lose myself in him," she says. "I'll wake up years from now, and I won't know who I am without him," she says.

"And is that so bad?" Saul asks.

"What will I do if I lose him someday?" She thinks back

to the day at the mines. She recalls the sheer terror she felt as she searched the men's faces for Caden's, and he wasn't there. "I can't imagine the thought of it, and he's not even mine," she explains.

"Loss is a part of life, darlin'. Nobody is guaranteed tomorrow or the next day. No one knows the number of days they are given except God. All we can do is live each day like it might be our last and be thankful if we have the opportunity to meet that special someone who makes us feel like they hold our world in their hands," Saul answers.

Jeri throws her arms around her uncle. "Why didn't we have this conversation yesterday before I ruined a perfectly good marriage proposal today?"

Saul holds her tight with his one arm while his other keeps a hold of his cane. "I didn't know my favorite niece was so dense," he teases.

"Thanks a lot, Uncle Saul," Jeri grumps.

"You're welcome, girlie. Now go get your guy," he orders.

"Yes, sir," she says before running out the door.

Jeri races to her car. She glances down at her phone, debating whether or not she should call Caden.

"Hey," she hears, and she stops in her tracks. She turns toward the sound of his voice.

"Hey," she answers breathlessly.

"Whatcha doin'?" Caden asks in a much lighter tone than he feels.

"I was...um... I was going to look for you."

"Why?"

"Because I made a mistake," she spits out.

"Oh? What's that?" he asks with a tiny bit of humor in his voice.

Jeri relaxes a little when she thinks there might be a little forgiveness there. "I said *no* when I should have said *yes*," she blunders.

"Is that right?" he says as he creeps closer. "Sounds like it was a pretty important question," he teases.

She drags a foot across the parking lot. "You could say that," she agrees.

He takes her by the hand. "I find I make the best decisions when I'm eatin'. You want to go get somethin' to eat?"

Jeri tugs him closer. She looks into his eyes. "For the rest of our lives?"

Caden's hand frames her face. He tilts her head back just a little as his lips meet hers for a slow, measured kiss that makes her feel like she's the only woman he's ever loved. "If you insist," he says when they come up for air.

"I do," she says before standing on her tiptoes to kiss him again. She tosses her arms around his neck and settles into him, hoping he accepts her apology for being so difficult. She lays her cheek on his chest. "I do," she vows. "I've followed you to work, to a funeral, and to the hospital, so I think it's fair to say I'm committed."

"I'm either signin' a marriage license or filin' a restrainin' order for being stalked," he teases.

"PFS or marriage license, huh?" Jeri muses. "I guess I'd have to go with a marriage license. I can't lose my job."

Caden holds her close. His chin rests on the top of her head. "Sounds like you made the right decision." His chin rests atop her head. "You think you can marry a criminal?"

"I've got a few get-out-of-jail-free cards up my sleeve," she says with a giggle as she gives him an extra squeeze. "We'll be just fine."

Don't miss out on your next favorite book!
Join the Melange Books mailing list at
www.melange-books.com/mail.html

———

THANK YOU FOR READING

———

Did you enjoy this book?

We invite you to leave a review at your favorite book site, such as Goodreads, Amazon, Barnes & Noble, etc.

DID YOU KNOW THAT LEAVING A REVIEW...

- Helps other readers find books they may enjoy.
- Gives you a chance to let your voice be heard.
- Gives authors recognition for their hard work.
- Doesn't have to be long. A sentence or two about why you liked the book will do.

about the author

I live in the beautiful Flint Hills of Kansas. I'm blessed to do two things I love- nursing and writing. I have wonderful family support including my husband, our son, daughter-in-law, and two daughters, my parents and in-laws, and too many more to mention as well as many friends who willingly give their input whenever it is requested. I'm thankful for the characters and stories as they come along, as well as the companies who publish them and readers who read them.

facebook.com/RachelAnneJonesAuthor

x.com/Jones1974Ra

instagram.com/diari197

tiktok.com/@idreamofdandelions

also by rachel anne jones

With Satin Romance

A Joy-Filled Christmas

Pickles-N-Fries and Fireflies

Stealing the Glass Slipper

A Stolen Heart

With Fire & Ice YA Books

Novels

Marmalade Uncapped

Essence of Emma

Lovestruck: Kisses, Lies & Oatmeal Cream Pies

All Or Nothing Series

Chasing Denver

Rough Terrain

A Firm Plateau

Radioactive Series

Love and Armageddon

House of Cinders

M.I.A.

The X-Factor